An Imprint of HarperCollinsPublishers

THE TEACHER

The Doberman was on a chain, which was attached to a runner that stretched the width of the yard. It had pulled the chain to its limit and could only stand in place, lunging helplessly but still barking.

A light came on, flooding the backyard. There was a movement behind the window in the back door.

At the very back of the yard, several feet from Lenny, was a wooden shack. Without even thinking about it, he ran for the shack, pulled the door open and ducked inside.

On top of a stack of wood was something long and black and shapeless and when he leaned closer, he saw that it was a black tarpaulin wrapped around something. With a sudden retching, he realized that a smell was coming from the tarpaulin. Taking a step back, he reached over and gingerly pulled a flap of the tarpaulin back a bit... a bit more...

More heart-stopping Nightmares...

Horrorscope *Nicholas Adams*
I.O.U. *Nicholas Adams*
Class Trip *Bebe Faas Rice*
Nightmare Inn *T.S. Rue*
Deadly Stranger *M.C. Sumner*

Joseph Locke

Lions
An Imprint of HarperCollins*Publishers*

First published in the USA in 1991 by
Bantam Books
First published in Great Britain in Lions in 1993
1 3 5 7 9 10 8 6 4 2

Lions is an imprint of HarperCollins Children's Books,
a division of HarperCollins Publishers Ltd, 77-85 Fulham
Palace Road, Hammersmith, London W6 8JB

ISBN 0 00 674759 0

Printed and bound in Great Britain
by HarperCollins Book Manufacturing Ltd, Glasgow

Once again, for
LOGAN TAYLOR
with much love

PROLOGUE

Word of Mr. Lehman's disappearance spread quickly, and by the time Christmas vacation was over, the students of Trenton Memorial High School had developed countless theories about their English teacher's possible fate. He'd been kidnapped; he'd left his wife to run away with a beautiful young woman, maybe a girl *their* age (after all, he *did* seem to be quite a flirt); he'd been in an accident and was wandering around with amnesia; or maybe he'd just gotten tired of the routine and had decided to chuck everything in favor of a new life in another town. There were many more possibilities, but those were the most popular.

No one at Trenton took any of the theories too seriously because no one really took Mr. Lehman's disappearance seriously. Of all the teachers on campus, Mr. Lehman was the hands-down favorite among the students. Even those who had performed badly in English in the past looked forward to Mr. Lehman's classes and, more often than not, did well in them. He taught with humor and understanding, something not often found in teachers of *any* subject, and students excelled in his class to please him, if for no other reason. He would be back, they were sure. He might miss a couple days, but he would show up with a smile and a chuckle and that just-kidding shake of his head, and it would be business as usual.

But they were wrong on all counts.

Mr. Lehman would not be back.

Because Mr. Lehman had been stabbed to death on a cold and rainy Christmas Eve.

And Mr. Lehman's killer would kill again. . . .

ONE

SPECULATIONS

"He's not back yet?" David asked as he slid onto a bench in the cafeteria, opening his brown bag and spreading his lunch before him in a quick but orderly way.

Todd shook his head, munching on Doritos.

"I'm telling you, he's dead," Lenny said smugly as he peeled an orange.

"Oh, come *on*," Teresa groaned, rolling her eyes. "Who would kill Mr. Lehman?"

Lenny stopped peeling to ask sincerely, "Who would kill *anyone*? I mean, who would *kill*? I still don't understand hunting, let alone murder."

"Oh, listen to this." Charlene laughed.

David barked, "Give me a break!"

Todd coughed back a laugh as he swallowed a mouthful

of chips and said, "Yeah! C'mon, Len, you love killing. What was the movie you brought over to David's New Year's Eve party?"

"*The Toolbox Murders*, and it's just a movie. That doesn't mean I love killing. Jeez." Lenny shook his head, smirking. He'd grown used to the ribbing, had even learned to enjoy it a little. After all, his tolerance of the teasing was one of the few reasons he'd been accepted into the most popular clique on campus.

"Listen to this." Todd laughed. "The guy wants to be Stephen King when he grows up, and he doesn't understand *hunting*." He bit into his turkey sandwich and talked as he chewed. "Between a Madonna concert and a mass murder, he'd buy tickets to the murder!"

Everyone laughed.

Everyone, except Pamela. She'd been toying with her salad, poking the lettuce with her plastic fork, frowning as the others laughed. Finally, she spoke up, but quietly: "I wish you guys would knock it off."

They all looked at her at once, startled by the sharp, serious tone of her voice.

"Something bad could've happened," she continued. "He could be hurt. Or dead. Maybe Lenny's right and somebody *did* kill him, how do *you* know? Crazier things are happening. Kids killing their parents, parents killing their kids. There are a lot of sick people out there. How . . . do you . . . *know*?" She started to take a bite of her salad but thought better of it and dropped the fork into the bowl.

Lenny's heart melted. He looked around at the others, then back across the table at Pamela. "I'm sorry," he said softly. "I didn't mean to make light of it. I wasn't joking."

"I know you weren't, Lenny, but they were." She turned to the others, fired up suddenly. "And you're all going to feel bad if it turns out that he *is* dead. I mean, why *else* would Mr. Lehman just disappear. It's got to be something bad, or he would've been here when vacation was over."

They all knew she was right and returned to their lunches silently. It was the first day of the second week after vacation had ended, and Mr. Lehman still hadn't returned; even his wife hadn't heard from him. They knew that something had to be wrong. Very wrong.

"I saw a cop in the administration office this morning," David said quietly, respectfully. "It probably had something to do with . . . well, with Mr. Lehman."

"Yeah, right," Pamela said. "You think cops would show up because he ran off with some fabulous babe? Something's *wrong*."

Lenny watched as her frown deepened; she continued prodding her salad aimlessly, and he winced at a pang of jealousy, wondering if she would be as worried if he were to disappear.

Of course she would, he thought, angry at himself for having such a notion. She'd be worried about anyone she knew. That's just the kind of person she is.

And Lenny was crazy about her.

Brushing aside a strand of her auburn hair, she lifted her eyes from the salad and looked at Lenny. The others at the table started talking among themselves. Lenny leaned toward her and spoke softly.

"I really didn't mean to joke about Mr. Lehman."

"Oh, I know, Lenny. I shouldn't have snapped. I just feel bad, I guess. I hear they've already found a replacement."

"What?" He couldn't believe it. It hadn't even been two weeks yet. Old Mrs. Bondurant had been sitting in for Mr. Lehman and they had been doing little more than busy work to pass the time until their teacher returned. If a replacement had been hired, then the school apparently had reason to believe that he *wouldn't* return. "Do you know who it is?" he asked in a whisper. The others at the table were already silent though, having overheard Pamela's news. They stared at her expectantly.

"I don't know," she said, "but it really doesn't matter, does it? Nobody's going to be able to replace Mr. Lehman."

They voiced their agreement with silence as they sat hunched over their food in the noisy cafeteria.

TWO

MR. TRANCAS

Lenny had English class right after lunch. He walked to class with Pamela, Todd, Charlene, Teresa, and David. Lenny looked out of place in this group, and a stranger who didn't know better would no doubt think he had simply fallen into step with them in the hall and didn't know them even slightly. A group photo could appropriately be captioned, *What's wrong with this picture?*

He was tall and lanky, and his dark hair defied styling. His thick-lensed glasses never quite rested comfortably on his face no matter how many times he had them adjusted. His love of films and novels in the horror genre was reflected in his collection of pins and buttons, one of which he wore today on the lapel of his blue and black plaid shirt; it read, in red dripping letters, "Come up and see my chainsaw." He had a crooked smile and a rather bookish face that simply did not fit in with the style of his friends.

The other guys—Todd and David—were both jocks. Although Todd spent most of his time with Charlene, and David spent most of his with Teresa, they could have had their pick of any girl at school. Both were blond and muscular and, even in January, sported the remains of last summer's tan.

Just as Todd and David could have had the affections of any girl, Charlene and Teresa would have been two of the most sought after girls if they had not already been taken by Todd and David. Both were cheerleaders; both were tall and slender—Charlene with fair skin and long blond hair, Teresa with short brown hair and big dark eyes that melted hearts with a single look.

Pamela, on the other hand, was unattached and, as a result, was probably asked out more often than any other girl at Trenton High. She, too, was a cheerleader. She was also a straight-A student who spent a good deal of time helping others with their homework. She was on the yearbook staff and worked on the school paper. She was, quite simply, a little too good to be true.

And Lenny—although he knew that he did not fit in the group, that he would normally be consigned to spend his time with the other nerds and misfits on campus, and that he probably had no chance whatsoever with her—did everything he could to spend as much time as possible with Pamela Anderson. The shocking thing was that she—as well as the others—seemed to enjoy his company.

But Lenny had a secret. He knew *why* they enjoyed his company. And it was okay with him.

They all stopped at their lockers in the hall, then filed into room 6A just seconds before the first bell rang.

The new teacher was seated behind his desk in front of the class, oblivious of the students coming in. He was paging through a folder of papers, looking down his nose through narrow reading glasses. He had a high forehead beneath his thin, neatly combed black hair, in which a few strands of gray sparkled under the fluorescent lights overhead. His eyebrows arched delicately above his dark eyes as he read, and the shallow hollows beneath his sharp cheekbones were like mere hints of shadow. He wore a brown corduroy sport coat, a rust-colored shirt, and looked a little like somebody you'd expect to see at your door handing out religious pamphlets.

As everyone began to take their seats he closed the folder and faced the class, smiling. He leaned back in his squeaky chair for a moment—

No, Lenny thought, *not his chair, Mr. Lehman's chair.*

—then stood as the second bell rang and stepped in front of his desk, his tall, lean frame standing straight and businesslike.

"My name," he said as he leaned back slightly on the edge of the desk, folding his arms again, "is Mr. Trancas. Gregory Trancas."

Lenny slumped down at his desk slightly. The skin at the back of his neck shriveled a bit. And he didn't know why.

"I, uh, know that I've come to you under rather unpleasant circumstances," Mr. Trancas said, scratching his cheek as he began to pace slowly in front of his desk, back and forth . . . back and forth, "but I hope that does not get in the way of our getting to know one another. I realize that I am replacing a teacher who has been here a good many years. And I understand that Mr. Lehman was—" He paused, chose his words. "—greatly admired at this school. Unfortunately, as I'm sure you all know, Mr. Lehman has disappeared. And his disappearance is, thus far, a mystery. But . . ." He stopped pacing, frowned deeply, and massaged the back of his neck for a moment. "I'm very sorry to tell you this, but the police have reason to believe that Mr. Lehman will not be returning to his position here at Trenton. So the decision has been made to hire a replacement. And that replacement is me."

A quiet murmur passed through the classroom, and Mr. Trancas waited patiently for it to die. When it did, he went on.

"Of course, that doesn't *necessarily* mean that Mr. Lehman has met with . . . trouble. He might very well surprise us all and appear just as suddenly as he disappeared. But in the event that he does not . . . I have been given charge of this class.

"Now, believe me, I will understand if you are reluctant to accept that fact. This is a jarring interruption in your routine. But, unfortunately, it is necessary, so here I am. I realize—" he removed his reading glasses, "—that I have some pretty big shoes to fill. That makes me very uncomfortable. So . . ." He smiled. "I'm not going to try to fill them. I am simply going to do my best to teach this class. I hope that you will understand my position and not expect me to emulate Mr. Lehman's teaching style. No two teachers are alike. I could not teach like him anymore than I could teach like any *other* teacher. I can only do this as I know best. I hope that you will be patient . . . and understanding . . . and open to my way of teaching the English language and literature."

Lenny looked around to see the others exchanging glances, some uncomfortable, some plainly disturbed—probably, he decided, hit hard with the sudden certainty that Mr. Lehman was gone for good. He turned back to Mr. Trancas, who was going on about the importance of understanding the English language. Lenny was disturbed, too, but about more than Mr. Lehman's disappearance.

What was it about Mr. Trancas that unsettled him?

His manner was a bit cold, but he was, after all, in an uncomfortable position. No, that wasn't it.

It was . . . *him*. It was Mr. Trancas. Lenny had seen him before, he was *sure* of it. But where. . . ?

". . . start by taking attendance," Mr. Trancas was saying, going behind his desk again. "Let's see, here . . . Benjamin Arliss?"

As he went down the list of names Lenny watched him, studying his face, trying to remember where he'd seen him—*if* he'd seen him, or was it just in his imagination?

He was certain it wasn't.

Lenny spoke up when his name was called, and Mr. Trancas looked directly at him with a flash of a smile, and once again, Lenny felt a twinge of discomfort that almost made him flinch. He closed his eyes, thought a moment, and . . . he could see him, Mr. Trancas, a fuzzy, grainy image of Mr. Trancas that, oddly enough, appeared in black and white in his mind's eye. Except it *wasn't* Mr. Trancas. Someone who *looked* like him, perhaps?

He opened his eyes and watched as the teacher stood behind his desk, opened his folder again, and scanned it with a frown.

That was it. *That* was what Lenny remembered, that frown—eyebrows knit together, lips bunched up, eyes narrowed, a thoughtful, concerned look—except it was in black and white and . . . and there was something else, something he couldn't put his finger on, something . . . *different*.

Mr. Trancas dropped the folder, stepped in front of the desk again, folded his arms, and said, "I think before we go any further, I should try to get to know you a little better. The best way to do that is for you to tell me about yourself. So, I'd like each of you to take out a piece of paper."

He began to walk slowly down the center aisle as notebooks slapped open and pages shuffled.

"I would like you to write a few paragraphs about your plans and hopes for the new year. You will have ten minutes." His footsteps tapped on the tile floor. Puh-*tap* . . . puh-*tap* . . . "You will not be graded for this. I simply want to acquaint myself with your abilities, your strengths and weaknesses. Please do *not* make a *list*," he added with a note of firmness in his voice. "Construct your paragraphs using complete sentences with proper punctuation and spelling."

The commotion in the room quieted as everyone began to write, and Mr. Trancas continued walking up and down the aisles. Occasionally, he would stop beside a desk and look over a student's shoulder at his or her paper, hands clasped behind his back, head bowed; sometimes he would point to something on the paper, speak quietly to the student; once, he stopped just behind Susan Chiklis, who was engrossed in her work, reached over her shoulder suddenly, and tried to pluck the pen from her fingers. When he couldn't, he said to her, "You're holding your pen too tightly." Then, to the class, firmly: "If you hold your pen or pencil too tightly, it will affect your penmanship." Another time, he stopped in the aisle and said, rather nicely this time, "Please remember the importance of posture. Sit up straight." Then his footsteps went on until he stopped again: puh-*tap* . . . puh-*tap* . . . puh-*tap* . . .

Lenny put pen to paper and began writing immediately. It was his strength. David and Todd were athletes; Lenny was a writer. At least he *hoped* to be a writer someday. He enjoyed making things up, weaving those things into a story, and putting them on paper. Writing came easily for him, and he welcomed an assignment like this one. There were several things he wanted to do in the new year. He wanted to get a subscription to *Fangoria* magazine, to which he hoped to sell a short story he'd written over Christmas vacation; he wanted to talk his parents into getting him a computer for his birthday in April; he hoped to finish the third volume of his scrapbook and start another by summer and . . .

His scrapbook. Filled with grainy black and white photographs from pulpy tabloids.

Lenny's hand stopped writing, and he felt cold suddenly; the back of his neck crawled with gooseflesh.

Put-*tap* . . . puh-*tap* . . . puh-*tap*.

A shadow fell over his desk. He heard slow breathing above him and a quiet "Hmmm." It took all of his strength to lift his head and look up at Mr. Trancas.

The man met his eyes and said, "Very good work.

But . . ." He looked at the paper again, read a few lines, and muttered, "*Fangoria?* Horror stories? Hmm. Pity."

Lenny watched Mr. Trancas walk away, hands clasped behind his back, shoes tapping on the tile, and when he looked down at his desk again, Lenny saw that his hands were trembling.

THREE

SUSPICIONS

Lenny and Pamela climbed into the backseat of Charlene's white 1969 Buick Skylark, while Teresa got in the front. As Charlene started the car she glanced in the rearview mirror and said, "Okay, the mall, right?"

The other two girls agreed, but Lenny said nothing. He didn't want to do anything but go home and take out his scrapbooks.

"Don't you want to go, Len?" Charlene asked.

"Huh? Oh, yeah, that's fine. I'll probably just walk home from there. I've got some things to do."

"In this rain?"

"I don't mind. It's not that far."

It had been raining all day, and the car's tires whispered through puddles in the parking lot as the wipers squeaked back and forth over the windshield. Charlene turned on the radio and found a Madonna song.

As they drove away from the school, a stranger watched them from the edge of the parking lot. He was tall, wore a dark raincoat and hat, and his left eye was covered with a black eyepatch. When they were gone, he turned his gaze toward the school itself. He stood there, staring, for a long time in the rain. . . .

"Something wrong, Len?" Pamela asked once they were on the road.

"Why?"

"You just seem so . . . preoccupied. Like something's bothering you."

"Oh, um . . ." He wondered if he should tell her. That blurry black-and-white image of Mr. Trancas had been eating at him all afternoon, and it would feel good to tell someone. But he knew it would sound weird . . . paranoid. His friends were accustomed to hearing strange things from him, but this was, perhaps, *too* strange. He'd keep it to himself. For now. "No," he said. "Nothing's wrong."

When they got to the mall, Charlene parked in the bottom level of the two-tiered parking lot. It was poorly lighted, and shadows darkened the gray concrete walls.

"Sure you don't want to go with us?" Pamela asked.

"No. I've got to go home," Lenny said.

Charlene got out, locked and closed her door, and looked over the roof of the car at Lenny. "Todd and David are going to meet us for burgers after practice. You want to come?"

"No, really." He held his books to his side and backed

away from the car. "I've got to go. I'll see you tomorrow, okay?"

They nodded and waved, and he did the same, then turned and headed for the street. He started up the hill that led to his neighborhood, his entire body tense. His fingers dug into the books he was carrying until his knuckles turned the color of milk.

Maybe he was mistaken. He *had* to be mistaken. He probably just hadn't gotten enough sleep last night. There had been a Karloff and Lugosi double feature on the late show, and he'd been up until four. Yes, that was it; he just needed some sleep.

The rain had lightened up by the time he reached his house. When he went through the front gate, his German shepherd, Champ, greeted him with a few jumps and barks. His mother was in the living room on the phone. She waved at him when he walked in, and he waved back as he headed for his bedroom. Once there, he closed the door, put his books on his desk, and pulled his scrapbooks from under the bed. He propped them up on his pillows and lay on his stomach to look through them.

Lenny's parents hated the scrapbooks. They were afraid that the books were a sign that he was becoming obsessed with death. He, on the other hand, had put them together as a sort of sociological project, the kind of thing that Lenny thought a writer would do. In fact, he got many of his story ideas from them.

The books were filled with newspaper articles, some of them from the local paper, others from national papers. All of the articles were about murders. Some concerned serial killings, while others—most, in fact—covered isolated incidents throughout the country, most of them bizarre in one way or another. One article told of a woman who pulled a gun out of her pocketbook and shot a department store clerk to death because the store had run out of her size in a particular style of shoe. Not all the stories were so morbidly humorous, though. Not the one he was looking for.

He found it on the seventh page of the second volume. The headline on the slightly yellowed newsprint read: **"HIGH SCHOOL STUDENT FOUND TORTURED, SLAIN."**

The article included a photograph.

Lenny leaned forward until his eyes were just inches from the clipping.

Could be, he thought, nibbling his lower lip. *Maybe. But . . .*

He got up and went to his desk, fished through the top drawer until he found his magnifying glass, and took it back to the bed, placing it over the picture. The caption beneath it read: **"Jonathon Grady, Spanish and vocabulary teacher at Piedmont High, said, 'Kathy had a limitless future ahead of her. What's happened is a shocking tragedy.' "**

Lenny held the magnifying glass over Jonathon Grady's face. He was bald on top with a fringe of hair on the sides of his head; he had a mustache, and the bowl of a pipe peeked over the edge of the breast pocket on his shirt.

No, he didn't look like Mr. Trancas. Not exactly. And yet . . .

There was a knock on Lenny's door as it opened quickly and his mother came in. "Leonard, did you *walk* home in this rain?"

He sat up suddenly, startled.

"Oh," she said, rolling her eyes, "and you've got *those* things out. Find another sick article? You know, your dad'll flip if he finds out you still have those things."

"I'm just . . . looking. I walked from the mall, that's all. It wasn't bad."

"Your hair's soaked. You should dry it off. Would you mind driving down to the store for me if I give you a shopping list? Your aunt Maggie's supposed to come over pretty soon, so I want to stick around."

"Sure. Can you wait a few minutes?"

"Mm-hm." She started out of the room, stopped, and turned again, looking at the scrapbooks and shaking her head disapprovingly before pulling the door closed.

Lenny returned to the picture, his forehead creased with a frown. He studied it for a long time, his eyes scanning Jonathon Grady's face carefully. As he did, a coldness spread slowly from the pit of his stomach.

Yes, his hair was thin. Yes, he was balding on top. He had a mustache and was perhaps a few pounds heavier.

But Lenny was certain that Jonathon Grady was Gregory Trancas.

FOUR

IN THE BURGER BARREL

Pamela bit into her cheeseburger as Teresa slapped David's hand away from her french fries.

"Hey, you've got your onion rings!" Teresa said.

"I changed my mind."

"Well, change it back."

The Burger Barrel was busy, as it usually was after school. The beef patties frying on the grill behind the counter whispered beneath the pounding of Janet Jackson's new song on the jukebox and the din of voices coming from the booths and counter. Pamela and the others sat in one of the rustic dark wood booths beneath a dim stained-glass swag lamp.

"Why didn't Lenny come?" Todd asked.

Pamela dabbed her mouth with a napkin and said, "Had something to do, he said."

"Something more important than *hamburgers*?" David chuckled.

Pamela shrugged and sipped her shake.

Todd leaned across the table and teased, "Y'know, Pam, Lenny's got a crush on you."

"So *what*?" Charlene said defensively before Pamela could respond. "I think it's kinda nice. And you don't mind, *do* you, Pamela?"

"Course not. Lenny's a great guy."

"Weird tastes and all?" Todd asked.

"Stephen King's made a lot of money off *his* weird tastes," Pamela said, cocking a brow.

"And how about Dean Koontz?" Teresa added. "Lenny's just more . . . imaginative than the average high school kid."

The boys looked at each other and rolled their eyes, and Todd said, "But you spend most of your time with him when you could be, you know, going out, dating. Chuck Strickland says he's asked you out twice now, and you keep saying no."

"I don't *want* to go out with Chuck Strickland," she said, wrinkling her nose.

David said, "He's Student Body president, for crying out loud. He's one of the—"

"—most annoying jerks at school, *that's* what he is," she interrupted.

Another moment of eye-rolling from David and Todd.

"Besides," Pamela said, "Lenny and I aren't *dating*. We're just really good friends who spend a lot of time together. I think he's got a lot more to offer than Chuck

Strickland." She sneered the name. "And so what if Lenny likes—"

She stopped when the door opened and Lenny walked in with a large book tucked under his arm. Pamela waved at him, and he hurried over and slid into the booth beside her.

Everyone greeted him as if he hadn't been the topic of conversation, and that made Pamela feel a bit guilty. She asked if he wanted a burger.

"Not hungry," he said quickly, a little out of breath. "Don't have time, anyway. I've got to get my mom's groceries home."

The boys rolled their eyes again, and Pamela scowled at them silently. "Is something wrong?" she asked.

"I . . . well, I'm not sure." He took off his glasses and wiped the speckles of rainwater from them with a napkin. When he put them back on, he looked around the table at them, as if he were about to say something, but remained silent for a long moment, apparently choosing his words carefully. Finally, he spoke. "Um, I wanted to ask you guys a question. Kinda stupid, maybe." He chuckled through a smirk. "But I'm just curious." He put the book on the table and opened it.

"Oh, no!" David laughed. "Not the death books!"

Todd bellowed, too, but the girls only laughed nervously, all three of them looking at Lenny with a hint of concern.

Lenny turned the book on the table so they could all see it and pointed to an article with a grainy black-and-white picture of a frowning man whose arms were folded and whose eyes looked off to his right.

"I'm just curious," Lenny said again, his voice trembling ever so slightly. "Does this guy look familiar to any of you?"

They all glanced at him to see if he was serious. It was obvious to Pamela that he was. They studied the picture for a while. Pamela put her elbow on the table and nibbled on her thumbnail as she looked at the balding, mustachioed man. She was so busy looking at him, in fact, that it took a couple moments for her to realize Lenny was covering the picture's caption with his hand. "Who is he?" she asked.

"That's not really important. Not yet. Does he look familiar?"

She nodded vaguely. "Sort of. I think."

"Yeah," Todd said. "He's one of those people who, you know, has a face that just looks kind of familiar."

"Mm-hm," Teresa added. "He's just got one of those faces. Like a million other people's."

"Who is he?" Pamela asked again.

"You don't recognize him?" Lenny asked again, ignoring her. "None of you?'

They all shook their heads. All but Pamela.

"Lenny," she asked, a little impatiently, "who *is* he?"

Lenny closed the book and shook his head, looking rather disappointed, frustrated. "Nobody important," he said quietly.

They were all silent a moment, looking at one another with confusion and concern.

"Well," Lenny said, standing suddenly and smiling, "gotta go. Mom's waiting for her groceries. See you guys tomorrow, okay?"

"Sure you don't want a burger?" Pamela asked quickly.

She wanted him to stay, to question him some more. Something seemed to be wrong.

"No, can't. Have a good night."

And he was gone.

When Pamela got home, she called Lenny.

"So, what's going on?" she asked.

"I'm eating dinner."

"No, I mean the picture. What was *that* all about?"

"Oh, nothing. Really."

"I don't believe you. You looked upset. Worried."

The line was silent for a while, then he said, "Tell you what. If you give me a day or so, maybe I'll tell you the whole story. Okay?"

"*What* story?"

He released a frustrated, uncertain sigh. "A day or so, Pamela. Please?"

She didn't like it, but she said okay anyway.

"I've got to get back to dinner. I'll see you tomorrow, okay?"

"Yeah. Okay. But if you want to talk—"

"I'll call."

She hung up, unsatisfied and a little worried.

FIVE

WINDOWS

"Directory Assistance, this is Karen, what city, please?"

"Dinsmore. Gregory Trancas." Lenny spelled the last name quietly so no one would hear him outside his bedroom. "And could I have a street address, please?"

There was a pause, then the operator gave him the address and a recorded voice gave him the telephone number. Sitting on the edge of his bed, Lenny jotted them down quickly in his school binder, then hung up.

He'd lied to Pamela. He'd had to. When she called, he hadn't been eating dinner. He'd excused himself from the table, telling his parents he felt a little nauseated and wanted to go to bed early. Instead of going to bed, however, he'd reread the article a few times.

He'd read again about the mysterious and brutal murder

of Kathy Marsden, a popular straight-A high-school senior in Piedmont, Oregon. Authorities believed her murder to be part of a pattern, the work of a traveling serial killer whose motives they did not yet understand. Three years before, there had been two similar killings in the state of Washington—one male victim, one female, both high school students with very promising futures—one in Walla Walla, the other in Seattle. Two years before that, two more had occurred in Great Falls, Montana. And, two years before *that*, there had been two in Wyoming. The authorities admitted they did not yet completely understand the killings but claimed they had evidence connecting all of them and predicted the next would take place in Idaho, where the proper authorities had been notified and were, according to the article, prepared.

He had articles chronicling a couple of the other killings—the one in Wyoming and the one in Washington—but there had only been pictures of the victims. He'd reread them anyway.

Then he closed the book and lay on his bed and thought about it awhile. If Mr. Trancas *was* the man in the picture, why was he now living in Dinsmore under a different name and with a totally different appearance? People only did that when they had something to hide. Did Mr. Trancas have something to hide? Would he squirm if he knew that Lenny had a newspaper article with a photograph that connected him to the Oregon killing?

Would he become dangerous?

Lenny went to the window and looked out into the night. The bushes and trees were blowing in the wind, but the rain had stopped. The cloudy sky held no moon or stars, and in spite of the streetlights, the night was dark.

He went to the door, opened it a crack, and listened. His parents were watching television in the living room. They were quiet, so that meant his dad hadn't started really feeling his booze yet. It would start soon, though. First, he'd yell at Lenny's mother, and if Lenny was handy, Dad would eventually get around to yelling at him too. Maybe he'd even rough him up a little. Unless Lenny was asleep. For some reason, even at his drunken worst, Dad respected Lenny's sleep. During the school months his father wouldn't wake him up, but in the summer, it wasn't uncommon for him to burst into Lenny's room in the middle of the night.

Lenny couldn't remember a time when his dad didn't drink every night. Sometimes he came home from his hardware store already drunk; Lenny suspected—was *certain*, in fact—that he kept a bottle in the back room of the store. It seemed to Lenny that by now he should be used to them, his father's drunken rages that would finally collapse into self-pitying sniffles and sobs as the man sat by himself in the living room until the late, late hours. It seemed that, since Lenny had known nothing else, his father's drinking would have become just another part of Lenny's life. But it hadn't. He *never* got used to it.

He closed the bedroom door, stuffed a pillow and some dirty clothes under the blankets on his bed until he had a shape that resembled his own, sound asleep. Slipping on his coat, he flicked out the light. Then he crawled quietly out his window.

The tires of Lenny's bike hissed over the wet pavement as he slowed a few houses down from 1215 Kelly Street. He got off the bike, lifted it onto the sidewalk, and leaned it against a tree, then walked the rest of the way to Mr. Trancas's house.

It was nine forty-five, and light still glowed in the windows. There were curtains on the side windows, while in front light shone through the thin openings of venetian blinds.

Lenny moved swiftly and silently across the front lawn to the largest window, then squatted down between two clumps of shrubbery. He raised his head slowly above the bottom edge of the window and peered through the narrow crack between two strips of gray plastic.

An icy wind murmured through the trees and shrubbery and passed over Lenny's back, but he didn't need that to feel a chill to the marrow of his bones.

Mr. Trancas, wearing a tan bathrobe, was leaning back in a recliner and reading a thick hardcover book. He held the book up in his lap with one hand; the fingers of the other were wrapped around the bowl of the pipe clutched between his teeth. A stereo in a cabinet behind him was playing gentle classical music. Steam rose from a mug on an end table beside him.

And the top of Mr. Trancas's head was completely bald.

"Oh, no," Lenny breathed.

He stared, openmouthed, through the window for several minutes before Mr. Trancas closed the book, put it on the end table, and stood, the pipe still sticking from his mouth, then walked out of the room. The light blinked out, and the room was plunged into darkness.

Lenny got up, his heart pounding hard in his chest. He chewed his lip, trying to decide what to do next. After a moment, he hurried around the corner of the house to the side window he'd seen earlier, hoping it was the right one.

It was.

He looked cautiously through a half-inch space between the curtains and saw an empty bedroom. Across from the bed was a dresser, upon which stood a Styrofoam plastic head, the kind a woman might place her wig on when it was not being worn. On this particular head rested a spidery black toupee.

Lenny felt his stomach sinking into his groin.

The door opened and Mr. Trancas—*No,* Lenny thought, *not just Mr. Trancas, but Mr. Grady, and who knows how many* other *names?*—walked in, scratching his bald head, yawning, his pipe in hand. He went to an ashtray beside his bed, tapped the bowl of the pipe into it, and turned to remove his robe. From somewhere inside the house, or perhaps in the backyard, a dog began to bark furiously. From the sound of it, it was a *very* big dog.

Mr. Trancas faced the window.

Lenny dropped to the ground, his back against the wall of the house.

I'm right, he thought. *Good Lord, I'm* right, *and nobody's ever going to believe me.*

The bedroom light went out after a moment, and Lenny hurried away from the house toward his bike, trembling.

It began to rain again.

DIAGRAMMING SENTENCES

Dinsmore was located about fifteen miles north of Eureka on the northern California coast. It was small, with a population just short of eight thousand people, and appeared to be one of those towns in which everyone knew everyone else. Most of the news was spread by word of mouth, making the weekly publication of the local newspaper little more than an obligatory gesture.

Most visitors were charmed by the town's seaside location, its lush greenery, windswept cypress trees, and mossy pines and cedars. There was one theater, the Vogue, which showed a third-run double feature every Friday and Saturday night, but most people drove into Eureka for entertainment.

The local teens hung out mostly at the Burger Barrel

and, in the summer, the Frostee Kone, which had outdoor tables; in the evenings, they parked at the Dinsmore Cove Lookout above the small cove, which was accessible by a long, steep, and crooked staircase that twisted down the cliff. There was a small park in the center of town frequented by small children and senior citizens.

Come sundown, Dinsmore became a dark ghost town. The foggy streets were virtually empty, except for the occasional evening stroller and those who had to make an unexpected run to the twenty-four hour 7-Eleven just south of town.

But people woke early, and most stores were open by eight, others no later than nine. As the sun rose and the mist from the sea dissolved, the streets and sidewalks, especially Cove Street, which was the town's main thoroughfare, became more and more active. Reverend Chalmers climbed the front steps of the steepled church at the same time every morning, unlocked the doors, turned to face the street, and took a long, deep breath before going inside. Lenny's father, Walter Cochran, would shuffle down the sidewalk to open his hardware store, his head hung low, shoulders slumped, still weak from his drinking the night before. Leo Waxner would open the Comicorner, jingling his keys as he whistled an elaborate tune. The schoolbus rumbled through town. Toddlers laughed in the park and sea gulls cawed overhead.

By shortly after nine A.M., the town was wide awake and alive, just as it was on this morning, the morning after Lenny's evening visit to Mr. Trancas's house.

Pamela knew something was bothering Lenny. She could tell by the way he'd been acting all day: quiet, withdrawn, wearing a troubled frown, and, strangest of all, jumpy. She spotted him standing at his locker at the beginning of the lunch period looking for something. Walking away from the others, she went to him and said quietly, "Okay, Len. What's on your mind?"

He jumped, startled by her voice, and a couple of books fell from his locker and clapped to the floor. "Huh?"

Pamela laughed and shook her head. "Why are you so jumpy?"

"I'm not jumpy. I mean, I didn't get enough sleep last night, is all."

"How come?"

"Because I was up late." It was almost, but not quite, a harsh snap. "Reading," he added, more gently. "I was reading."

"Lenny, are you sure nothing's wrong? You really don't seem yourself."

He stopped and stared into his locker for a moment, then looked around to see who was nearby and if anyone was paying attention. He whispered, "Do you have any plans after school?"

"Not really. I'm supposed to pick up my sister from a late band practice later, but I'm—"

"Could we go into Eureka?"

"Sure. What for?"

"I want to go to the library. There's something I'm looking for, and I can't use my parents' car today."

"Okay. We'll go after school. Let's go have lunch now, okay?" She was concerned. There was something a little too frantic about the way he'd asked her to take him to the library.

"No. I'm . . . not hungry. Really. I'll see you in English." He picked up the books, tucked them under his arm, and closed his locker, then headed down the hall.

He's skipping lunch? she thought. That *really* worried her. . . .

"Today," Mr. Trancas said after taking attendance, "we're going to be diagramming some sentences. Having looked over his schedule, I see Mr. Lehman had not yet covered sentence diagramming in much depth, so I thought it might be good for us to start out by covering some new territory." He went to the long green chalkboard and, on the left side, began to write a column of sentences.

Oh, no, Lenny thought, his back stiffening. *He's going to have us go up there and diagram those sentences.* Lenny enjoyed English because he loved to write and enjoyed working with words; his skill, however, was more instinctual than academic, and when it came to something as technical as diagramming a sentence and labeling its different components, he had little confidence in his abilities.

Besides, Lenny did not want to go up there and stand next to Mr. Trancas. *Or Mr. Grady, or whoever the heck he is,* he thought. In fact, he didn't even want to be in the *room* with Mr. Trancas, even though he had no solid reason for his discomfort. Not yet. He hoped to find his reason at the library in Eureka.

"You," Mr. Trancas said, gesturing Arthur Bell to the board to diagram the first sentence while asking the boy his name. Arthur was hesitant, his hand trembling as Mr. Trancas looked on, his lips tight, brow wrinkled, and head shaking with disapproval. When Arthur was finished, Mr. Trancas nodded toward Arthur's seat, silently telling the boy to sit back down. "Anyone *else* care to give this sentence a try?" he asked. No one volunteered, so he pointed to Carrie Waterman. "Your name, miss?" he asked. She told him as she went to the board, even more timidly than Arthur, now that she could see the stern expression on Mr. Trancas's face.

Once again, Mr. Trancas shook his head and gestured for her to return to her desk.

"I'll try it," Pamela said.

Lenny flinched at the sudden change in Mr. Trancas's expression. His frown disappeared, and he smiled broadly, nodding as he said, "Yes, Pamela. Go ahead." He kept smiling, arms folded over his chest, posture straight with confidence, as if he *knew* she would get it right.

Of course, she *did* get it right. Pamela usually got *everything* right, and on the rare occasion she made a mistake, she made it only once. She breezed through the sentence, diagramming it perfectly.

"Very good, Pamela," Mr. Trancas said quietly; it was almost a whisper, brimming with satisfaction and approval. "Go ahead and do the next one."

She did.

Mr. Trancas's smile grew, and his eyebrows rose high. "*Very* good, Pamela," he said in that same gentle voice. "Mr. Lehman hadn't covered diagramming much yet. How is it that you did this correctly and with such ease?"

She shrugged as she dropped the chalk back in the tray. "I read ahead a little in the text."

Mr. Trancas's eyes took on a strange look then: they narrowed slightly and looked at Pamela the way one might look at a thing of wonder—a flawless diamond or a perfect, unbroken rainbow. Then he whispered, "Thank you, Pamela. You may sit down." Moving slowly, he went behind his desk, locked his elbows, pressed his big hands on the desktop, and leaned forward, looking at the class.

"I hope you all heard what Pamela just said. She read ahead in the textbook. I'd like you to keep that in mind. On occasion, I might jump ahead a bit and spend a period covering a topic we've not yet studied at length. I do this from time to time to keep you on your toes. I'm very concerned about the amount of apathy I find in so many students today. So many fail to realize that being a student is a great thing . . . a *noble* thing. Because a student is someone who is learning. *Growing*. Someone who is absorbing information and skills that will make him or her a better person, that will improve the quality of his or her life and will open new doors, create new opportunities that might not otherwise have been available. Learning is a tremendous thing. It is something that should be craved, not simply tolerated."

He stood there, leaning over his desk, and looked at them for a long time, his eyes passing slowly back and forth over the class. He looked at them long enough to make them squirm, Lenny included.

It was an odd speech for a teacher to make suddenly . . . and so deadly *seriously*. Something else struck Lenny as being odd. This was only Mr. Trancas's second day, and he hadn't had time to learn everyone's name by heart; he'd had to ask Arthur and Carrie for their names.

He'd known Pamela's name immediately.

Big deal, Lenny thought, trying to chide himself for his groundless, senseless suspicion. *It's nothing. He just happened to remember her name. She's pretty, she stands out in any class.* But Lenny still could not dissolve the nagging lump of tension in his chest.

"Now," Mr. Trancas said, suddenly ending the long, uncomfortable silence, "if you'll just open your textbooks . . ."

SEVEN

LENNY TELLS HIS STORY

"This is *crazy*," Pamela hissed in the silence of the library.

"Maybe, maybe not," Lenny whispered, concentrating on the microfiche reader. Newspaper articles swept across the screen, then stopped, swept by some more, then stopped again as he searched for one particular article.

"So he remembered my name from yesterday," she went on. "What does that mean?"

"I don't know. Yet."

"*Yet?* Well, when do you think you'll—"

"Here it is."

Pamela watched as Lenny read the article, then scribbled notes in his notebook. His hand froze, and his eyes widened slightly as he stared at the screen.

"Look . . . at this," he breathed.

The article included a picture of three adults and one teenager. The caption identified the teenager as a friend of the victim and the adults as three teachers at Oakmore High School in Great Falls, Montana.

Lenny pointed to the man on the right.

"Him," he said. "Does he look familiar?"

Pamela looked, instead, at Lenny. A look of near panic showed on his face. What had gotten into him? Had their old joke—that someday, after too many horror movies, novels, and comic books, Lenny would start to *believe* in all of that stuff—finally become a reality? After hearing his story on the way over—that he suspected that Mr. Trancas was not who he claimed to be and that maybe, just *maybe*, he'd been involved somehow in a number of killings—she wondered quite seriously if that were the case.

Lenny saw that she wasn't looking at the picture and whispered, "Come on, Pamela, look at this guy! Doesn't he remind you of someone?"

She looked. The man had bushy hair and a full but nicely trimmed beard. Although it was hard to tell because of the picture's graininess, it looked as if the man's mustache covered a scar on his upper lip, perhaps the remnant of a cleft palate.

"You've *got* to be kidding, Lenny," she said, getting impatient.

"Just look closely. Please."

She studied the picture again, just to satisfy him.

"Look at the eyes," he said. "And that expression. See how far his eyebrows come down over his eyes when he frowns?"

"But what about the scar on his lip? Mr. Trancas doesn't have a scar."

"Makeup."

"What?" Pamela shrieked, and slapped her hand over her mouth immediately, looking around at the disapproving faces of the other people in the library. Whispering, she repeated it: "What? Are you out of your mind, Lenny? You think Mr. Trancas goes from school to school disguised as a different person, using makeup and changing his name? Why would he want to do that? And what's made you *think* such a thing?"

He turned to her, his expression very serious now, serious and hesitant.

"I didn't tell you everything," he said.

"Everything about what?"

"About Mr. Trancas. I didn't tell you what I found out about him last night."

The slight tremble in Lenny's whispered voice and the intensity in his eyes frightened Pamela a little. Now she wondered not only what had gotten into Lenny, she wondered what *he'd* gotten into. What had he been doing? Sneaking around? Spying?

"Well," she said, "maybe you *should* tell me."

"I want to make a few more notes and make sure I've gone over everything here about the murders. Then I'll tell you in the car."

I can't wait, she thought. But the dryness of her throat and the nervousness in her stomach would not allow the thought to be a sarcastic one.

It was raining again, and the wipers on Pamela's old VW bug squeaked horribly as they *shooshed* over the windshield. To Pamela's left, down below the road at the foot of a cliff, the ocean raged, slamming its foamy waves against the black, jagged rocks, sending sea gulls screeching into the air. As she drove back to Dinsmore, she listened carefully to Lenny's story of his secret visit to Mr. Trancas's house the night before.

"That was stupid, Lenny," she snapped. "Just plain stupid. What if you'd gotten caught, huh? How would that have made you look, huh? Like some *sickoid pervo*, that's what."

"But I *didn't* get caught, Pamela. And I saw something." He leaned closer to her in the seat. "He's bald. Mr. Trancas is *completely bald* on the top of his head. And . . . he smokes a pipe." He said it in the same tone of voice he might have used to tell her that Mr. Trancas lived in a spaceship and levitated above his bed as he slept.

Pamela's mouth dropped open in disbelief. "Lenny, I really think you should see a doctor. And I *don't* mean an M.D."

"But don't you see the connection?"

"Connection to *what*?"

"The article in my scrapbook. Mr. Grady was bald on top. And *he* smoked a pipe too. It's sticking out of his shirt pocket in the picture."

"Do you know how many bald men in the United States smoke pipes? What's wrong with you, Lenny?"

His shoulders slumped, and he turned away from her with a look of childlike disappointment.

"This is a joke, right?" she asked, smiling. "Just a story you've made up, right? Like last year when you had us all convinced that there were rituals and sacrifices going on late at night inside that old abandoned house? Remember? You went in there ahead of us that night and scattered all that fake blood around and hid those big bloody knives?

And you put black candles all over the place and hung that huge pentagram on the wall? You scared the pants off us. So, that's what this is, right?"

"No." He shook his head wearily. "No, *that* was a joke. *This* . . . is real. Why do you think I'm telling just you? I knew the others would laugh. I thought you'd listen. But I guess I should've known you'd laugh too."

"Lenny, don't say that. I'm not laughing at you, really. I just think you're getting yourself worked up over nothing. Maybe you *shouldn't* spend so much time collecting all those weird newspaper articles and reading those books. I mean it. You think about that stuff too much."

"He was a Spanish and vocabulary teacher in Oregon."

"What?" she asked, confused.

"Mr. Trancas. Er, Mr. Grady, I mean. The guy in the picture I showed you yesterday. And the guy we saw on the microfiche? He taught literature and spelling. And I think—I don't care *what* you say—I think there's a physical resemblance. It's something about the eyes, the expression . . ."

"Oh, I'm not saying there's no resemblance. But some people just have familiar-looking faces, y'know? And what does it matter what they teach?"

"Don't you get it? They're all related. English, Spanish, vocabulary, literature, spelling? And in the article about the killing in Walla Walla, Washington—the first one we looked at—they interviewed a guy who taught English *and* vocabulary. His name was—" He checked his notes. "—Lawrence Tanner."

"But that doesn't mean anything. There wasn't even a picture. And besides, Lenny, you *still* haven't told me what this is all about. Why would Mr. Trancas *do* this?"

"Because maybe he's got something to hide. Maybe there's something he's running from." Lenny paused, then turned slowly to face her. "Maybe . . . maybe *he* killed all those kids."

She just sighed and shook her head slightly.

"Think about it, Pamela. They were all straight-A students. Top of the line in their schools. All really talented with big futures ahead of them. College, degrees, great careers planned. And, Pamela . . ." He paused for a long time then. ". . . he likes you. I can tell by the way he looked at you, the way he spoke to you today. And, like I said before, he knew your name when he called you to the board, he didn't even have to *think* about it."

"So *what*?"

"What do you mean, 'So *what*'? Everybody knows, Pamela, you're the biggest brain on campus. You're involved in most of the clubs. You've got a career in journalism all planned out already. Pamela," he whispered, "you're a straight-A student."

In spite of herself, gooseflesh crawled down Pamela's back like an army of ants.

EIGHT

MORE PICTURES

Lenny rode his bike to school the next day armed with a plan. He'd faked a note from his mother saying he had a dental appointment during fourth period P.E.—he'd gotten pretty good at forging his mother's handwriting, although he seldom used it—and gave it to Mrs. Potter, the secretary in the office, when he arrived. That gave him fourth period and lunch to carry out his plan.

When the bell rang at the end of third period, he hurried out of the room and out to the parking lot before Pamela or any of the others could see him and ask where he was going, then got on his bike and rode into town. He parked in front of Comicorner, the store where he bought all of his horror novels, comics, and magazines, and went inside.

"Leo," he called.

Leo Waxner was behind the counter unloading a box of new comic books. He was an enormously fat man with long, stringy gray hair and a Santa Claus-like beard. He clutched a short, stubby cigar between his teeth. "Hey, kid," he said, "you should be in school, shouldn't you?"

"I'm at the dentist's right now."

"Hah!" Leo bellowed.

There were no customers in the store, just as Lenny had hoped; there hardly ever were during school hours. "I need a favor, Leo. Well, three favors, actually."

"Will it cost me anything?"

"Three long-distance phone calls, but I've got money to pay for them." He removed a piece of paper from his jacket pocket and unfolded it. He'd written it the night before. "I want you to call three schools, two in Washington State and one in Wyoming. You'll probably get the office secretary. I want you to tell her this." He handed the paper to Leo. "Go ahead, give it a run-through."

Leo frowned, looked at Lenny, and said, "Is this something illegal?" Lenny shook his head. "Is it important?" Lenny nodded. "But you don't want to tell me about it." Lenny shook his head again. Leo cleared his throat and began reading. " 'Hello, my name is Edward Lansdale. I'm a journalist, and I was wondering if you could give me a little help with a piece I'm doing for the San Francisco *Chronicle*.' "

"Now, this next part," Lenny said, "is what you tell her if she asks what the piece is about."

" 'It's a feature about how people change their looks as the times change. I was going to focus on young people, you know, teenagers. But I decided it would be more interesting if I focused on teachers and faculty instead. We know students keep up with trends, but do *teachers*? That's what I'd like to find out. If it's not too much trouble, I'd like you to photocopy some pages from one of your yearbooks and fax them to me. I'd like the faculty portrait sections from . . .' Wait a second, you left a blank space here."

"Yeah, that's where you say the year. I want a different year for each school."

"Where are these gonna be faxed to?"

"Two doors down at the Copyman."

"Mm." He nodded. "Well, how do I sound?"

"Well, let's go through it a few times. Try to relax, sound more natural. Okay?"

Leo shrugged, pulled up a chair, cleared his throat, and began to read again.

Leo did a fine job. The school in Walla Walla did not have access to a fax machine and couldn't help, but Seattle and Wyoming agreed without question and were even pleased to know their schools were going to be mentioned in the article.

Afterward, Lenny paid Leo and hurried two doors down to the Copyman. He told the young blond girl behind the counter that he was expecting two faxes within the next few minutes. Then he waited.

When they arrived, he paid for them without looking at them, folded them up, put him in his jacket pocket, and went across the street to the Burger Barrel. It wasn't until his burger arrived that he took the sheets out, unfolded them, and examined each of the pictures.

By the time he'd taken two bites of the burger, he had found the pictures he'd wanted. He stared at them for a long time, then got up and paid for his burger. He'd suddenly lost his appetite.

When he noticed the time, he ran to his bike, opened his book bag, and stuffed the yearbook pages into his binder.

He was late for English.

When Lenny entered the classroom, it was silent. Mr. Trancas was pacing up and down the aisles as he had done the first day. Lenny eased the door closed quietly but did not escape being noticed. A few heads turned toward him. And Mr. Trancas stopped and turned around, one brow cocked.

"Sorry," Lenny said. "I had a dental appointment. The office knows about it."

Mr. Trancas thought about that a moment, then nodded. "The assignment is on the board. Take your seat. And in the future, I would appreciate it if you'd schedule your appointments for *after* school." He turned and continued walking up the aisle.

Lenny's heart hammered beneath his ribs as he went to his seat. He put his books on the desk top, and as he removed his jacket his arm struck the books and they began to slide off the desk. As they slid, Lenny's breathing came to a halt.

The faxed photocopies of the yearbook pages eased out of his binder.

He nearly fell reaching for them but was too slow. The books and binder hit the floor with a *smack*, and the pages scattered over the floor, whispering against the tile.

Lenny couldn't move.

He couldn't breathe.

He looked at Mr. Trancas, who stood less than a yard away up the aisle. The man turned, hands behind his back, brow cocked again, eyes dark with disapproval, and looked down at the floor. He moved forward, holding his arms out to help Lenny pick up the books.

"N-no," Lenny said, his voice hoarse as he dropped to one knee and began to scoop his things up frantically. "That's all right, I-I've got 'em. Really. I've got 'em." He slapped both hands over the yearbook pages, crumpled them a little, and stuffed them back into the binder, then stacked his other books on top of it. His knees trembled as he stood and then sat down behind his desk. He looked up at Mr. Trancas, who was leaning toward him, lips moving as he spoke. Lenny could hear nothing, however, but the throbbing of his heart and the rushing of blood, like thunder, in his ears. All he caught was, ". . . gas you . . ."

He blinked, confused and afraid. "I'm sorry?"

"I said," Mr. Trancas repeated quietly, and a little impatiently, "did your dentist *gas* you? You're acting a little strange, if you don't mind my saying."

"No, I don't mind. I-um, I mean, no, just, um, just a lit-little Novocain is all."

Mr. Trancas nodded, standing straight, hands behind him again. He looked at Lenny for a long moment, his eyes darkened by the shadows of lowered brows. Then he turned and walked. Puh-*tap* . . . puh-*tap* . . . puh-*tap* . . . up and down the aisles. Up and down, up and down. . . .

NINE

SKEPTICISM

"I *know* you didn't have a dental appointment," Pamela whispered as they left Mr. Trancas's room. "What's *wrong* with you? You look like you've seen, I don't know, a *ghost*, or something."

"A ghost I could live with," he said, looking around suspiciously and glancing over his shoulder.

"What's the matter?"

"Come here. Before the others catch up." He clutched her elbow, took her around a corner, and they ducked into the library.

"I'm going to be late for Music Apprecia—"

"It'll only take a sec."

Most of the other students in the library were gathering their things quietly to head for their next class, but a few remained seated, oblivious of the bell, hunched over open books and binders.

"Is this more of your crap about Mr. Trancas?" Pamela asked as they sat across from one another at one of the long tables. She was beginning to get angry.

"Just listen." He opened his binder, pulled out a few pages, and handed them to her, reaching over and pointing to one of the many small square pictures on the page. "David Witten. He taught reading and vocabulary at Lincoln Junior High School in Seattle, Washington, where Lynda Crawford and Peter Dunleavy were murdered one year apart." He pulled out another page and put it on top of the stack, pointing to another picture as he whispered, "Andrew Duncan. He taught spelling and English at Faraway High School in Wyoming, where Kitty Brock and Corey Jennings were both murdered, a year apart." He leaned closer. "Now look at those two men. Look *closely*."

Frowning, her eyes shifted back and forth between the two pictures. "You're crazy," she said simply, trying not to sound angry, though her anger was building. "Look, this one—" She pointed at Duncan. "—this one looks like he might be Hispanic. He's *dark*, his hair is black, and he's—"

"But look at the *face*, Pamela, just the face. Forget the hair and the wire-rimmed glasses and just look at the face, the eyes."

She clicked her tongue, shook her head, and pointed to the other one. "This guy's heavier. Quite a *bit* heavier, I mean, this is rid—"

"They were all straight-A students, Pamela. Just like you. And in three of the articles about these killings, *he* is questioned and always says the same thing about them. He says—"

"He, *he*, what do you *mean*, he? They're all different men."

"But he—"

"No!" she snapped. "I don't want to hear any more of this. You've really gone too far with this, Lenny." She took a deep breath, softened her harsh tone. "I know you're upset about Mr. Lehman disappearing like he did. We all are, Lenny. But we've got to give Mr. Trancas a chance now. And, you know, I actually kind of like him. He's a little stiff at first, kind of stern. But he's a good teacher. Very thorough and smart. I think we could *all* come through this class with good grades if we listen to him, *let* him teach us, and . . . and if you wouldn't insist he's some kind of psycho-killer."

His face fell as he leaned back in his chair, defeated. She was genuinely surprised by the look of overwhelming disappointment—and was there some dread there too?—that darkened his features.

She whispered, "You're really . . . *serious* about this?"

He didn't answer at first.

"I mean, it's really just one of your jokes, isn't it?"

Nothing; he just stared at her sadly.

"Lenny? Isn't it?"

His head moved slowly back and forth, and he breathed a single word: "No."

The bell rang, and she waited for him to get up, but he didn't move. "C'mon," she said, standing, "I'm late. Walk with me."

She went to his side, but his eyes remained on the spot

where she'd been sitting. He shook his head again. Pamela almost asked him if he was all right, but she didn't have time, and frankly, she was fed up with his little B-movie plot. She had to admit that, at first, it had given her a chill. Lenny could always do that, and she knew that, someday, he'd make one heck of a horror writer. But he'd gone too far with this one. She really *did* like Mr. Trancas, and he seemed to like her. Of course, David and Todd taunted her about being the teacher's pet; they were *always* doing that. Pamela knew she was a good student, and that was not just a conceit. She had good study habits and worked hard, and usually she ended up being a sort of "teacher's pet" in most classes. Mr. Trancas was no different than any other teacher. And he *certainly* wasn't a serial killer.

Pamela ruffled his hair and said, "See you later, Lenny," then hurried to class.

Lenny felt exhausted. He hadn't gotten enough sleep, that was for sure, but that wasn't the reason.

He was so sure—so dead solid *certain*—that he was right and had tried so hard to prove it to Pamela, that her refusal to believe him—to even *listen* to him—was a tremendous drain of energy. And the heavy, burning feeling in his gut that something was brewing, that something was going to happen that would put Pamela in danger, didn't help at all.

Lenny got up, put the pages back in the binder, and carried his books out of the library, stopping just short of the door when something caught his eye. It was a handwritten sign taped on the wall to the right of the door:

FACULTY
DINNER MEETING
TUESDAY NIGHT
7:00 P.M.
FACULTY DINING ROOM
ALL FACULTY MEMBERS ARE
REQUESTED TO ATTEND
DON'T FORGET!

A faculty dinner, Lenny thought, staring at the sign. *And they're all supposed to go. That means . . . Mr. Trancas will be out of his house for a while.*

And so, Lenny decided as he left the library, would *he* . . .

THROUGH THE WINDOW

"It's going to be a stoooorrmy night, so gather 'round your radio and stay warm—no, make that *hot*—with Paula Abdul . . ."

Lenny turned down his stereo and locked his bedroom door, muttering, "No *kidding* it's gonna be a stormy night."

His father had come home from work drunk, plopped into his chair in front of the television, and had gotten up only a couple times since to go to the bathroom. He'd even skipped dinner, as he usually did when he'd had enough liquor to kill his appetite. That was fine with Lenny; he'd eaten in peace with his mother at the kitchen table then had gone straight to his bedroom.

It was just past six-thirty; the faculty dinner would start

in about half an hour. That gave him plenty of time to get a few things together: a pocketknife, a small flashlight, and one more thing.

He left his bedroom quietly and stood in the hall a moment. He heard his dad coughing and muttering in the living room—he was still watching television and not likely to move soon—and his mother was washing dishes in the kitchen. Moving quickly, he took a few steps down the hall and ducked into his parents' bedroom.

He spotted it immediately on the bookshelf: their small black Nikon One Touch 100, lying right beside its leather case. Just as he closed his fingers around it, the telephone rang.

Lenny rushed out of the room on the balls of his feet and returned to his own room just as his mother called, "Lenny, it's for you."

His heart was racing as he picked up the receiver. "Hello?"

"Hi, it's me," Pamela said. "You okay? You sound . . . shook up, or something."

"I'm fine. Just ran to the phone."

"Oh. Look, I wanted to apologize for today. I think I was a little hard on you. I really didn't mean it. I just wanted you to, you know, get off that whole thing about Mr. Trancas."

"Yeah. Well . . . don't worry about it."

"You sure you're okay?"

"Yeah, I'm—"

A burst of shouting came from the living room and a door slammed: his parents' bedroom door. Lenny froze, thinking his father had discovered the camera missing. But it was just another drunken rage that had, as usual, come out of nowhere. The shouting continued—complaints, curses—and Lenny closed his bedroom door quietly.

After a moment, Pamela asked, "Your dad? Again?"

"What do you mean, 'again'?" Lenny chuckled coldly. "You mean, *still*, don't you?"

"Sorry. I wish things were different for you over there."

"Well . . . they're not." He was embarrassed that Pamela had heard the shouting. She'd heard it before, but it *always* embarrassed him.

"Tell you what," she said. "Let's go see a movie. I'll even go to one of those horror things, if you want."

"No. But thanks."

"You sure?"

"Yeah. I've got some things to do."

"Oh. Okay. Well . . . you sure everything's all right? I really don't like the way you said that. *What* things?"

"Some reading," he lied. "Homework." Before she could ask him which class the homework was for, he wrapped up the conversation quickly, but politely, and said he'd see her tomorrow.

Then, he thought, *I hope.*

He put on his jacket and put the camera in his pocket after checking it for film—there were seven pictures left—then donned his rain slicker and rubber boots, picked up his umbrella, and went to the kitchen. "Can I borrow the car for a little while, Mom?"

"You're not going out in this *rain*, are you?" she asked, turning off the faucet and drying her hands.

"I have to. I've gotta get to the library before it closes." Another lie.

"But you haven't been driving *that* long, Leonard, and

the weather's supposed to get worse tonight. Can't you just—"

"Let him go!" his father yelled from the bedroom. "He wants to have a wreck in the rain, what do *we* care? We got insurance!"

His mom closed her eyes and sighed, then said, "The keys are in my purse. Don't be too late."

"Thanks." He started toward her to give her a kiss, but she'd already gone back to washing the dishes and frowning. He got the keys.

On his way out of the house, Lenny glanced at a portrait of himself and his parents on the living room wall. It had been taken a few years ago. He sat between them and they each had a hand on his shoulder. All three of them wore big smiles. They looked so warm, so happy.

Lenny hated that picture.

The disc jockey had been right; it *was* a stormy night. The wind was blowing hard—so hard that Lenny had to clutch the steering wheel in his fists to maintain control of the Olds—and the pounding rain fell at a slant so hard and fast that, even on high speed, the wipers barely kept up. Lenny drove more carefully than he ever had before; what would he tell his parents if he had a wreck going in the *opposite* direction from the library?

Motley Crue was on the radio, but he turned it off; heavy metal was not exactly relaxing, and if he needed to do *anything* at the moment, it was to relax.

A block from Mr. Trancas's house, Lenny turned off of Kelly Street and onto Bertram and parked in front of an empty lot. His stomach was fluttering as he unfolded his foot-long umbrella and held it over his head, walked around the corner, and headed for the house.

The porch light was on, and there was no car in the driveway. Of course, it could have been in the garage, but Lenny suspected Mr. Trancas was gone by now. He looked around to make sure there was no one nearby who might see him trying to break into the house, then quickened his pace.

He stopped at the corner of the front yard and ducked behind the shrubs that surrounded it so he could observe the house from a small distance before trying to get inside. In spite of the umbrella, the rain slapped against his slicker with the sound of a dozen machine guns firing at once.

Where would be the best place to start? In the glow of the streetlight across the street, he could see that there was a basement window just above the ground beneath the front window. It was awfully narrow and a little too visible for comfort. Maybe the bedroom window he'd looked through the last time he was here was a better idea.

He only hoped the dog he'd heard wasn't *inside* the house.

Crossing the lawn quickly, he ducked under the small overhang above the bedroom window, collapsed the umbrella, and tucked it into his jacket pocket beneath the slicker. The house seemed dark inside. As he removed his pocketknife and opened it he took another quick look around, just to be sure no one was watching, then tried the window. It was locked, as he'd suspected. He slid the blade of his knife between the aluminum frames of the two panes, scraping, scraping, until he felt it pop through. Then he slid it underneath the latch.

It was a trick he'd learned as a small boy. His parents

insisted on keeping all doors and windows locked at night so, whenever he wanted to get away from his dad but had nowhere to go, he would walk through the living room, undergo the usual shouts and insults, and pretend to leave; but he actually went around to his bedroom window and broke back in, then lay in bed and read undisturbed. Of course, back then, he'd never latched the window tightly, so his trick always worked.

This time he wasn't so sure.

He jiggled the blade until it stopped against the latch, a solid barrier. Pulling the blade back a couple inches, he tried again. And again. He felt the latch loosening and kept at it. On the eighth try, the latch moved aside stubbornly, and he was able to lift the sash, only a few inches at first, then all the way up.

Lenny removed his rain slicker and tossed it on top of a rosebush to the left of the window, then turned around and hiked himself up onto the sill to remove his rubber boots. He'd thought ahead about it; if he went into the house with his dripping slicker and muddy boots on, he would leave tracks all over the place. So he decided to leave them at his point of entry and put them back on as he left. Squeezing his knees to his chest, he turned around on the sill very carefully and stepped inside, closing the window behind him. He took his flashlight from his jacket pocket and switched it on, inspecting his surroundings.

There was a neatly made double bed to the right, an impeccably organized bureau against the opposite wall, and a half-open closet to the right of that. Colors were gone in the small beam of his flashlight; it was like standing in the middle of a black-and-white photograph.

He stood there for what seemed a long time, just looking around, until it finally hit him:

Exactly what are you looking *for?* he asked himself silently.

He wasn't sure. Not yet. But he was certain that if he looked hard enough, he'd know it when he found it. He started with the nightstands that flanked the head of the bed.

The first held a pipe, an ashtray, a lamp, and a couple of paperbacks. There was a lamp on the other one, too, along with a number of hardcovers stacked neatly, all of them textbooks on various subjects: English, literature of all sorts, Greek mythology, art, calculus, biology, ornithology, chemistry. Out of curiosity, Lenny returned to the other nightstand and checked the paperbacks. They were both written in Spanish.

Jonathon Grady taught Spanish, he thought.

Getting down on one knee, Lenny took a picture of the paperbacks, then did the same with the hardcovers on the other side, making sure the titles were plainly visible.

Behind him, the opposite wall was almost completely covered by a floor-to-ceiling bookcase filled with rows of hardcover volumes. Lenny went to it and ran his light along one of the shelves. More textbooks and countless stuffy-looking books that covered everything from philosophy to the study of insects. Half a dozen of the books, fat, intimidating ones, were each about a single scientific theory. Two shelves held nothing but classics, some of which were in foreign languages.

He turned, sweeping the flashlight beam through the room again, and noticed something even more odd than Mr. Trancas's reading material. There were no pictures in the room. There were none hanging on the wall, none standing on the bureau or nightstands. In fact, except for a single painting—a tacky piece of work depicting an ocean scene, the kind of thing you might see in a motel room or a waiting room—the walls were completely bare. Quickly, he checked everywhere—under the bed, the dresser drawers, the nightstand drawers, the closet—but found absolutely nothing one wouldn't expect to find in such places. In fact, judging from the contents of his drawers and closet—and especially from the contents of his bookcase—Mr. Trancas appeared to be a very neat but incredibly boring man.

The hallway was a bit more normal; framed photographs lined the walls, pictures of babies and children, brides and grooms, and smiling old men and women, some framed individually, others grouped in collages. There was something oddly familiar about them—not the people but the pictures themselves, their style and *look*—that gave Lenny the same kind of déjà vu feeling he sometimes got when he walked into a room he knew he'd never seen before. It took him a little while, but he finally figured it out. At least . . . he thought he'd figured it out.

The people in the pictures were too perfect. There were no fat people on the wall, no mussed hair or sloppy clothes, no ugly faces . . . not even any average faces. Everyone looked quite perfect, like models. Even the pictures themselves were flawless: perfect composition and focus, clear as water, each with a very professional, staged look to it.

In fact, they looked like the kind of pictures that were put in frames for display on store shelves: anonymous, attractive people in somewhat average, familiar settings, but with just a touch too much perfection to be real family photographs.

The wind raged outside, blowing rain against the windows as Lenny looked at the pictures.

He carefully removed a picture of a beautiful young woman from its hook, removed the cardboard backing from the frame, and pulled out the photograph.

But it wasn't a photograph. Not a real snapshot, anyway. The picture was on very thin, slick, shiny paper, the kind of paper magazine pages were made of; it did not have the texture or sturdiness of a photograph. And printed on the white back of the flimsy picture in small black letters was:

SIZE–8 × 10
MADE IN TAIWAN

Lenny replaced the picture and removed another, a wedding shot.

It was exactly the same. He didn't bother checking any of the others; he knew they would all be alike.

Staring at them, thinking about them, made him shiver. What kind of person had no *real* photographs on his wall, only store-bought pictures of fake friends and relatives?

A sick *one,* he thought, *that's what kind.*

His mouth was cotton dry, and he realized he was breathing harder and faster. Taking a deep breath to calm himself, he headed down the dark hall with only his flashlight beam to guide him. He stopped at each door, checked each room.

The bathroom held nothing interesting.

The next room held nothing. It was completely bare, even the closet. Lenny suspected it was meant to be a spare bedroom, but Mr. Trancas had obviously left it untouched since moving in.

He went on, passing through the dining room. Nothing out of the ordinary there. The living room was ahead through the next doorway, but it revealed nothing about Mr. Trancas that Lenny didn't already know. The room was so neat and tidy, it looked as if no one lived there, and the furniture was bland, nondescript, with a television, a modest stereo system, a clean fireplace, and a short bookcase that held a few paperbacks. Lenny went to the bookcase and inspected them. They were all bestsellers, none more than six months old, and not a single one of them looked as if they'd been touched. Most of them, in fact, still had the bookstore's price tag stuck to the cover.

A sort of disguise, perhaps? Had Mr. Trancas bought the books as decoys, props to put in his living room for the benefit of any visitors who might come over, showing them that he, like everyone else, read Robert Ludlum and Mary Higgins Clark and Dean R. Koontz and Sidney Sheldon and all those other writers who seemed to stick to the bestseller lists like Scotch tape to paper? Judging from the books in his bedroom, all of which looked well-used, Lenny figured that was the case.

He went into the kitchen. His beam passed over cupboards, an immaculate counter and sink, a refrigerator without a single magnet or note on the door, a stove, a microwave, and . . .

There was a piercing shriek from the dark, just to Lenny's right, and he swung around, blurting out a frightened, "Oh, my gosh!"

"Oh, my gosh! Oh, my gosh! Craw-*craaawwk*! Oh, my gosh!"

The light from Lenny's flashlight fell on a white cockatoo in a cage hanging from the ceiling.

Lenny stumbled backward and bumped into the lip of the counter, leaning heavily on it as he heaved a sigh of immense relief. Once he'd regained his posture, he approached the cage, looking up at the bird, and said quietly, "Hi, fella."

The bird squawked again, then said, "Reading writing! *Craaawwk!* Reading writing! Reading writing and 'rithmetic!"

Lenny frowned. "What's your name, huh?"

"*Craawwk!* Board of education!"

Frowning even more, Lenny made a kissing sound with his lips and said, "Huh? What's your name?"

"A mind is a terrible! Craw-*craaawwk*! A mind is terrible thing . . . *crawk!* . . . to waste!"

Lenny just watched then as the bird fidgeted in its cage going back and forth between the two perches.

"Work to do!" it squawked. "Plenty . . . *crawk-crawk!*. . . . plenty of work to do! Little monster! Let the . . . *craaawwk!* . . . let the little monster have it!"

Lenny gulped, licked his dry lips, and backed away from the bird.

"Board of education! Craw-*craawwk*! Let the little monster have it, *crawk*!"

They certainly weren't the words of the average talking pet bird. Lenny had heard of parrots, minah birds, and cockatoos reciting nursery rhymes, profanity, and things like "Polly wants a cracker," but *this*? Birds usually said the things they heard most often. Were these the words of Mr. Trancas . . . or whoever he really was?

"Probably," Lenny breathed with a chill.

Beside the refrigerator, a door opened onto a laundry room, and beyond the washer and dryer was another that probably led to the garage. To the left of the laundry room, a door opened onto the backyard—Lenny could see through the window in the top half—and to the right, just beneath the bird's cage, was another door.

The basement, Lenny thought, opening the door. Beyond it lay darkness even more dense than that he'd been walking through in the house, and disappearing into that darkness was a wooden staircase.

The steps creaked beneath his feet as he descended slowly into the blackness. The air was damp, and the concrete floor was veined with cracks. Overhead was a tangle of intestinelike pipes, and the walls were plain Sheetrock. Lenny ran the light over the walls, noticing that something wasn't quite right.

There was no window.

He was *sure* he'd seen a rectangular basement window outside, and he went to the place he thought it would be. There *was* a window, but it had been boarded up. Tacked to the boards that covered the window was a campaign poster for George Bush with a photo of him standing against a stark white background, looking very serious and presidential, staring off to his right, as if in deep thought. At the top, written in red letters, was:

THE EDUCATION CANDIDATE

At the bottom in blue letters:

THE EDUCATION PRESIDENT

Below the poster and against the wall was a cot with a thin pad to serve as a mattress, two pillows, and some blankets folded neatly at the foot. A makeshift nightstand—four cinder blocks stacked beneath a square piece of plywood—stood beside the head of the cot with a few papers and a blue folder resting on it.

A door near the corner to Lenny's right opened onto a cramped bathroom. Boxes were stacked against all four walls of the basement, and there were books stacked on some of those. Lenny started toward a group of boxes but stopped when he bumped into something in the center of the room.

It was a school desk, the old kind with a wooden top that lifted up to reveal a compartment beneath it for books and papers. The desk top had darkened with age and was marred by scratches and nicks.

How did I miss this? Lenny wondered. After all, it was in the center of the room, facing one of the front corners.

But it was no *ordinary* old school desk. Two armrests had been built onto the chair's wood-slatted back, each with a hinge so it could be folded up or down, and something else . . .

Straps. Each armrest was equipped with two strong leather restraints about half an inch thick.

Lenny lifted the desk top. There was nothing inside but stains. He held the light closer. They were old and crusty, and he thought, for a moment, that they were nothing more than rust. But on closer inspection, he realized he was wrong.

When he scraped a fingernail over the blotchy stains, they sloughed off easily, unlike rust, which was much more tenacious. When he rubbed his thumb and forefinger together, the dry, reddish-brown substance flaked away in tiny crumbs.

"Blood," he whispered.

Old blood that had been shed on the desk some time ago. He wondered to whom it belonged, or if perhaps the splotches were a mixture of blood from several victims. The two in Washington? In Wyoming, maybe? He really didn't want to think about it . . . but he couldn't help himself.

Lenny backed away from the desk a step, jaw slack, and began to walk around it slowly when his head bumped something above him. He looked up and gasped.

Two heavy cables, with a manacle at the end of each, hung from the web of pipes. The cables were each looped over a pulley and continued across the room diagonally, toward the corner that the desk was facing, and wound around a spool, a sort of makeshift winch, with a crank.

A small, sickened groan crawled up from Lenny's chest.

With trembling fingers, he removed the camera from his jacket pocket, pulled back the top half of the case, and took pictures of the desk—one with the desk top open, one with it closed—then of the manacles and cables, and one of the winch, leaving only one shot in the camera. He would have to choose well.

Feeling a bit queasy after allowing his mind to entertain Mr. Trancas's use of the manacles, Lenny turned and went to the boxes along the wall.

Books. More books.

Then he found something that looked unfamiliar. One of the boxes was filled with a stack of dark blue vinyl-covered folders. They looked like . . . diplomas?

He set the camera on the stacks of boxes to his left,

took out a folder, and opened it under the flashlight. It *was* a diploma, but not from any school he'd ever heard about. . . .

This is to certify that

____

has successfully completed the requirements of
this institution and is hereby awarded this
Diploma as a certificate of graduation from
The School of Thought.

____

__________________ __________________

Date *Principal*

He went through several others in the box. They were all blank and looked brand-new, untouched. He moved to the next box and opened it. More diplomas. But these were not blank.

The first looked as if it had been handled a great deal. It was made out to Lynda Marie Crawford. Lenny blinked a few times, calling up the name. She was one of the victims in Seattle. The blank space marked "principal" had been signed: David Witten. That was the name Mr. Trancas had assumed in Seattle.

Lenny's heartbeat quickened as he opened the next folder. It was made out to Peter Garrett Dunleavy, the *other* Seattle victim, and also signed by David Witten.

The next folder he opened looked older, worn, and the parchment was yellowed and speckled with faint stains. It was made out to Michael Pritchard and signed by Professor Duncan E. Wexton. The names were not at all familiar to Lenny, and he dropped it, went on to the next.

It was made out to Katherine Alice Bancroft and signed by Jonathon Grady.

When he opened the next one, he dropped it to the floor as if it had bitten him. The parchment inside was spattered with old blood. Shining the flashlight beam on it, he saw that it was signed by Andrew Duncan, Mr. Trancas's Wyoming name, and made out to Kitty Brock.

A lump rose in his throat. Mr. Trancas actually made out *diplomas* for his victims? Then it struck him: the folder on the cot's nightstand. Lenny dropped the diploma back in the box and hurried to the nightstand, got the folder, and read it as he walked back to the boxes against the wall.

He froze halfway there. For a moment, he couldn't breathe. He stared at the diploma with his mouth gaping.

It was signed Gregory Trancas.

It was made out to Pamela Lynn Anderson.

"Pamela," Lenny whispered. He put the diploma on the boxes and held it open as he lifted the camera, aimed, and snapped the picture. Putting the camera down again, he stared at Pamela's "diploma" for a long, terrified moment, then quickly opened the next box.

He found what appeared to be a plain brown photo album with a handwritten label that read: **"YEARBOOK."** Inside were twelve snapshots that took up the first three pages. They were pictures of miserable looking teenagers, boys and girls, who looked pale and unhealthy and terrified, with mussed, unwashed hair and sunken cheeks. Beneath each picture was the teenager's name handwritten in neat block letters. None of them were smiling. Except one . . .

His photo was older, with yellowed borders, and it was in black and white. A healthy, smiling boy, clean-cut with straight teeth and bright eyes. The name beneath it was Wesley Coswell.

Lenny had recognized most of the names; they were the victims he'd read about in the newspaper articles. But there were others he'd never heard of before. And the black-and-white photo of the young man was especially puzzling. It was too old to be included with the others. Who was Wesley Coswell?

Lenny took in a breath to whisper *Oh, my gosh,* but there was a sound that made his stomach twist into a knot.

A car outside. It was faint, but unmistakable. The car slowed to a stop. The engine fell silent. A car door opened.

And Lenny could hear someone whistling a cheerful tune.

Mr. Trancas was home.

ELEVEN

TRAPPED!

Lenny didn't have time to put everything back where he found it. He had to get out!

He dropped the "yearbook" into the open box before him, spun around, and bounded up the stairs. There was no way he could climb them quietly; they were too creaky, and his feet clunked on the wooden steps. He reached the top, opened the door a crack, and listened.

Mr. Trancas was still outside the house whistling happily, but his footsteps had stopped, and Lenny could hear keys jingling.

He would be inside any second.

Lenny shot out the door, closed it, and went across the kitchen to the back door, but his stocking feet slid to a stop on the tile floor.

He could hear scratching on the other side of the door. Scratching and whining. It was the dog he'd heard the night before last. The *big* dog . . .

If he went out there, he figured he had a pretty fair chance of being mauled by whatever dog was big enough and strong enough to make that door shake as if it were being rammed, just by scratching it.

He heard the front door open.

The cockatoo startled him with a loud, "*Crawk!* Oh, my gosh! *Craaawwk!*"

"Hey, Woodrow!" Mr. Trancas called to the bird from the living room.

Lenny's terror was so overwhelming that, for a moment, he thought he was going to scream, just throw back his head and shriek at the top of his lungs. He forced himself to move instead and ducked into the laundry room as lights began to come on in the living room.

The door that he supposed led to the garage had a chain lock on it and he knew he wouldn't have the extra second or two it would take to unlock it because now he could hear Mr. Trancas whistling his way through the dining room. Moving as quickly and quietly as he could, Lenny slipped into the narrow utility closet next to the locked door and closed it, only vaguely noticing the mop, broom, dust pan, and rags hanging all around him as he turned off his flashlight.

"Oh, my gosh!" the bird squawked. "Craw-*craawwk!* Oh, my gosh, oh, my gosh!"

"Oh, my gosh?" Mr. Trancas laughed. "Where did you get *that* one, Woodrow? Huh?"

"Craw-*craaawwwk*! Little monster! Little monster! *Crawk!*"

Lenny held his breath, trying to tell himself that *of course* the cockatoo was not trying to warn Mr. Trancas of his presence in the house.

He heard Mr. Trancas's footsteps moving around the kitchen, heard the refrigerator open, the pop and hiss of an aluminum can being opened, then heard the refrigerator door close.

"Left the meeting early, Wood," Mr. Trancas said. "And do you know what I told them?"

"Little monster! Little monster!"

"No, no," he laughed. "I said I still had some unpacking to do, some things to move. 'Mostly dead weight,' I told them." Then he burst into a fit of belly laughs. "How do you like *that*, huh? I said I had to move some dead weight, *hah*! If they only knew, huh, Woodrow?" His laughter faded as he left the room, but Lenny could hear his whistling drifting through the house.

Mr. Trancas returned to the kitchen and said, "We've got a lot of work to do, Woodrow. We have to prepare for our new student."

Lenny's blood chilled. He knew who the new student was going to be.

"Maybe a little cleaning up would be in order. I'll get that garbage out of the shed—" He chuckled. "—and later, I'll go to the—"

The telephone rang.

"Woodrow! It must be the phone!" Mr. Trancas said jovially, and his laughter trailed behind him as he left the kitchen once again.

Lenny listened to Mr. Trancas as he talked on the telephone. He couldn't make out the words, but from the tone of voice, it sounded as if Mr. Trancas was settling into the conversation, as if it might be someone he had been waiting to hear from, or someone he hadn't spoken with in a while. Whoever it was, it sounded like a conversation that was going to take a little while.

After listening for a few more minutes, Lenny decided he might have just enough time to take a shot at getting out. If he went into the garage, he might not be able to get out without opening the garage door, which would be noisy; he wasn't sure if there was another door leading outside. As frightening as it was, his best bet would probably be to go into the backyard and run as fast as he could, and just hope he could outrun the dog.

It's now or never, he thought, easing the closet door open. He was thankful that he'd taken off his boots—which he would have to retrieve along with his rain slicker before he went back to the car—because they would have made too much noise, but he wasn't looking forward to going out into the cold, rainy night in his socks.

He crept into the kitchen and went to the back door and turned the deadbolt slowly, silently.

"Oh, my gosh! Oh, my gosh! *Crawk!*"

Lenny jumped at the bird's cry.

". . . just my bird," he heard Mr. Trancas say in the living room.

"Little monster! Craw-*craaawwwk*! Little monster!" The bird flapped its wings furiously, making its cage swing back and forth; Lenny glanced over his shoulder to see a few white feathers fluttering to the floor.

He turned the knob slowly, then quickly pulled the door open just enough for him to squeeze through, and pulled it closed quietly behind him. He walked a few paces away from the door until he was standing in the rain, then turned on his flashlight and . . .

The light glinted off two black, vicious eyes and illuminated a black-and-brown snout that came just above Lenny's waist, and a mouth opened up to flash two rows of yellowed fangs that snapped at him as the Doberman let out a string of roaring barks.

Lenny's shock came out as a small gurgling sound in his throat. He ran as fast as he could over the grass, his socks soaking through immediately, his flashlight beam bobbing and sweeping through the night as the dog chased him. He could actually hear the Doberman's fangs clacking together with each bark. He could feel the dog closing the distance between them and finally resigned himself, even as he ran, waiting to feel the dog's weight as it pounced on him, waiting to feel its teeth and claws.

But suddenly the dog's barking was silenced with a single startled yelp, and the rapid pad of its feet on the wet ground stopped, replaced by the metallic jangling of a chain.

Lenny glanced over his shoulder, then stopped completely and turned.

The Doberman was on a chain, which was attached to a runner that stretched the width of the yard. It had pulled the chain to its limit and could only stand in place, lunging helplessly but still barking.

A light came on, flooding the backyard. There was movement behind the window in the back door.

Lenny looked around frantically, horrified by what he saw. The yard was surrounded by a wooden fence that was well over six feet tall, and he couldn't see a gate!

At the very back of the yard, several feet from Lenny,

was a wooden shack. Without even thinking about it, he ran for the shack, pulled the door open, and ducked inside.

Wood was stacked inside, leaving him just enough room to stand absolutely still. Above the pattering sound of rain and the dog's barking, Lenny could hear Mr. Trancas.

"What's going *on* out here, Teddy? Huh? What are you so excited about, boy?"

The dog's barking calmed and became a frustrated whine in response to its master's question.

There was a small knothole in the door of the shed, and Lenny hunkered down to put his eye to it.

Backlit by the lights that shone from the edge of the overhang above the back porch, Mr. Trancas stood with hands on hips, surveying the backyard. His head moved slowly to the left, then to the right, then back, his gaze stopping on the shed.

With a gasp, Lenny flung himself back away from the hole, his back pressing against the damp stack of wood behind him.

Mr. Trancas said, "You want a snack, Teddy? Huh? Would you like that? Will that calm you down?"

The dog replied with a low, throaty *woof*, and then Lenny heard the sound of a spoon scooping dog food out of a can.

After a few minutes, the lights blinked out, and darkness settled on the backyard.

It wasn't until Lenny had calmed somewhat and his ears were no longer filled with the drumming of his heart that he noticed the smell in the shed. He hadn't smelled it outside, but inside it was enough to make him wrinkle his nose and stifle a few thick coughs. The smell reminded him of sour milk . . . no, it was worse; it was more like the smell of rotting meat, and the more he smelled it, the worse it seemed to get. He covered his nose and mouth with one hand as he took his flashlight from his pocket with the other. Curling his fingers around the end of it to dim it and keep it from being seen, he flicked it on.

There were some yard tools hanging on the walls—rakes, shovels, a hoe, and a pick—and the rest of the shed was taken up by the stacked wood. On top of the stack was something long and black and shapeless, and when he leaned closer, he saw that it was a large black tarpaulin wrapped around something, and he realized with a sudden retching that the smell was coming from that tarpaulin. Taking a step back, he reached over and gingerly pulled a flap of the tarpaulin back a bit . . . a bit more . . . and more still . . . and . . .

Lenny cried out into his hand as he dropped the flashlight and fell to his knees, trying not to be sick.

It was Mr. Lehman.

On hands and knees, Lenny groaned again and again, teeth clenched and eyes closed tightly. His stomach was rolling, and a lump had grown in his throat.

I'll get that garbage out of the shed, Mr. Trancas had said. . . .

It took him a while, but with slow, deep breaths, Lenny finally managed to relax—a little, anyway—and think.

A picture, he thought. *One picture of this and* nobody *will say I'm crazy. Just one pic—*

But he had no pictures left. He'd taken the last one in the basement.

And then it hit him like a fist to the kidney.

He'd left the camera in Mr. Trancas's basement.

His first reaction was to cry, but he blinked back the

stinging tears. He had taken only seven pictures; what *else* was on the roll of film?

Christmas pictures, of *course*, left over from the holiday. Pictures of his parents, pictures of *him*.

Shaking his head sharply, as if to clear it of the nightmarish thoughts that were screaming behind his eyes, Lenny allowed himself to think only of getting out of the shed, out of the yard, and back to the car.

He picked up the light, turned it off, put it away, and stood slowly, feeling a little dizzy. Without looking at Mr. Lehman's body again, he opened the door cautiously . . . a little more . . . a little more . . .

When there was no reaction from the dog, he stepped out, closed the shed door, and moved toward the fence. Wind blew rain in his face, and no matter how careful he was, his feet made sloshing noises on the muddy ground. At the fence, he reached up to grasp the top and heave himself over but immediately jerked his hands back, hissing painfully. Something had scratched his fingers. He reached up again, cautiously this time, and found barbed wire. It had been placed all around the top of the fence on the inside to keep people out . . . or in.

Probably both, he thought.

Feeling his way along the fence, he finally found the gate, which was locked with several bolts. Throwing them all carefully, quietly, he stepped out of the backyard and closed the gate.

Once he had his boots and rain slicker, he hurried back to the car, not bothering to put them on.

TWELVE

LOST AND FOUND

By the next morning, the rain had turned to a mild, misty drizzle, and Lenny rode his bike to school. He didn't feel like sharing anyone's company yet. In fact, he'd considered not going to school at all.

Rather than getting any sleep, he'd merely dozed the night before, and those rare moments were haunted by nightmares that jarred him awake in a sweat.

What was he to do? Go to the police? He had no proof now; his pictures were locked in his camera down in Mr. Trancas's basement. And even if he *did* manage to convince the police to look into it, what good would it do? They had no grounds on which to search Mr. Trancas's residence. And if they talked to him and found him suspicious, Mr. Trancas would have plenty of time to hide all the incriminating evidence before they were able to search the place.

Frustrated, helpless, and exhausted, Lenny decided to go to school and do the best he could. But the thought of going to English class made him sick with dread.

"I haven't seen Lenny all day," David said at lunch. "Is he home sick or something?"

"I've seen him around," Teresa replied quietly, "but he wasn't in biology."

Frowning, Pamela said, "He's here. But something's wrong."

"What?" Charlene asked.

"I'm not sure, but I think it's got something to do with his dad. I was talking to Lenny on the phone last night, and I could hear him yelling in the background."

"Oh, him," David said, rolling his eyes. "What a case *he* is. The guy drinks like a fish. I don't know if he still does it, but, when we were kids, he used to beat up on Lenny. On Mrs. Cochran too."

"Yeah," Todd agreed, nodding. "It's been pretty tough for Len. I'm surprised his dad's still alive, the way he drinks. His liver must be a chunk of granite by now."

"I don't know why Mrs. Cochran's stayed with him as long as she has," Dave said. "She should've left him years ago, when Lenny was a kid."

Teresa said, "Well, some people are like that, y'know."

Todd slapped Dave's arm and said, "Yeah, come on, man, don't you watch Oprah?"

The boys laughed.

"This is serious," Pamela interrupted. "I think it's gotten worse, maybe." Quietly, half to herself, she added, "I think that's why he's gotten so caught up with this crazy idea about Mr. Trancas."

"What crazy idea?" Teresa asked.

She hesitated at first, thinking about it awhile, then told them of Lenny's suspicions about their new English teacher.

"A *killer?*" Todd laughed. "*That* guy? He's too much of a *dweeb* to be a killer."

"I can see the headlines now," Dave said, grinning. "English Teacher Murders Student for Dangling his Participle!"

The boys laughed again.

"Come on, you guys, cut it out," Pamela chided. "This is serious, *think* about it. Of *course* it's a crazy idea—Mr. Trancas being a killer, I mean—but why would Lenny keep harping on it like that? Why would he be so determined to convince me it's true?"

"Because that's what he *does*," David replied. "When we were kids, he had Todd and me convinced there was a monster living in an underwater cave just below the cove. We stayed away from there for *months*! We were scared to *death* of the place!"

Todd said, "Yeah, he loves scaring people, *you* know how he is. And he's *good* at it too."

"But I think this is different," Pamela persisted. "I think maybe he's just doing it to get some attention. Because of the way things are at home. Or maybe he's so upset that he actually thinks it's *true*. I mean, for a little while, there, he almost had me convinced. At least I considered it for a little bit. No, this seems different. I don't think it's just one of his jokes, one of his stories."

"You think it might be true?" Charlene asked, puzzled.

"Of course not! I just think it's a bad sign, a sign that

Lenny is very upset. Maybe more upset than even *he* realizes. I think that maybe . . ." She looked down at her untouched lunch, feeling a little guilty for what she was about to say. ". . . that maybe he needs some help. Some counseling."

"He'd never go for that," Todd said flatly, biting into a sandwich.

"I know," Pamela replied. "That's why I'm thinking about talking to Mr. Elliot about it."

Mr. Elliot was one of the school's counselors, the only one who was actually a psychologist.

David frowned. "You think that's a good idea? I don't know if Lenny would appreciate that."

"Maybe not. But I think he needs help. I know he might not like it, but—" She took a deep breath and sighed. "—I'm going to do it, anyway."

Lenny's stomach had not felt very strong, so he'd avoided biology, nauseated by the idea of dissecting a cow's eye. He hadn't been hungry, either, so instead of the cafeteria, he'd gone to the library and read. Well . . . he hadn't actually read anything, just looked blindly at a lot of pictures and illustrations.

When the bell finally rang, a shudder passed through him that no amount of control could have hidden, and he actually saw his hands quake on the table before him.

The walk to English class was long and miserable, and although he was surrounded by other students in the hall, he felt completely and utterly alone.

When he walked in and took his seat—just seconds before the final bell—he did not look at Mr. Trancas. He kept his eyes down, staring at his desk top. In the silence that followed that last bell, his mind flashed on the desk in Mr. Trancas's basement . . . the battered old wooden top . . . the dried blood underneath. . . .

Mr. Trancas said, "There are ten sentences on the board. All of them include errors in either spelling, punctuation, or grammar. I would like each of you to take out a piece of paper and do two things. First, rewrite all of the sentences, correcting the errors; second, diagram each sentence. You'll have the entire class period. At the end of class, pass your papers to the front."

There were a few quiet groans as the rustle of notebooks and papers filled the room, then there was only the occasional whisper of pens and pencils writing busily.

Lenny couldn't avoid it; he had to look to the front to see the sentences on the board . . . but he *didn't* have to look directly at Mr. Trancas. And he didn't. From the corner of his eye, though, he saw the man sitting at his desk, apparently reading or looking at something.

Fighting to concentrate on the assignment, Lenny began to write.

Less than ten minutes into the class, a crackle of static came over the public address system, and everyone, including Lenny, looked up at the speaker on the wall.

"Good afternoon, students," Mr. Walsh, the principal, said as he cleared his throat.

It was unusual for him to make an announcement so late in the day, and curiosity clouded the eyes of everyone in the class.

"As you all know," Mr. Walsh continued hesitantly, "Mr. Lehman has been missing for a few weeks now. Well, I have some . . . some sad news to report. This morning at nine fifty-two A.M., Mr. Lehman was . . . Mr.

Lehman's *body* . . . was found on the rocks just north of the cove."

There was a long silence on the speaker as gasps rose from the class. A couple of the girls began to cry.

With an emotional tremor in his voice, Mr. Walsh said, "The cause of death has not yet been determined. In light of this tragedy . . . school will close for the remainder of the day."

More sobs erupted in the room.

I'll clean that garbage out of the shed, Mr. Trancas had said.

And that was exactly what he had done.

Lenny realized he was digging his fingers into the underside of his desk . . . so hard, in fact, that his fingertips ached.

"But before you go, I would like to say that . . . well, this is going to have a powerful effect on us all, faculty as well as students. Mr. Lehman was a teacher here for almost eight years, and he will be missed greatly. I would like to say that no one . . . *none* of you should be ashamed of your feelings. I would encourage all of you to talk about this. Talk with one another . . . talk with the faculty. Feel free to share your feelings. We should *all* feel free to . . . to mourn our loss. I've spoken with Mr. Elliot, and he has informed me that his door will be open. He encourages drop-ins from all of you. No appointment necessary." Mr. Walsh paused, then said, "Classes are now dismissed until tomorrow morning."

The P.A. clicked off.

"Well," Mr. Trancas said quietly, almost reverently, but Lenny still did not look at him. "This assignment can wait. I think it would be inappropriate to give you any homework for tonight. I'm . . . terribly sorry for your loss. I'll see you all tomorrow."

There was a loud clamor—louder than usual with all the crying—as everyone closed their books and stood to leave.

Mr. Trancas coughed loudly. It was a forced, artificial cough. It wasn't until then that Lenny lifted his eyes and looked at his teacher.

Leaning back in his chair behind his desk, Mr. Trancas looked directly into Lenny's eyes. His face was tense, ominous, his mouth a thin straight line.

And before him in his hands, he held a small stack of snapshots.

An ice-cold fist struck Lenny in the chest. He staggered to his feet, gathered his things, and so horrified he could not even *think*, he hurried clumsily out of the room.

THIRTEEN

THE MOURNING AFTER

Mr. Elliot was a diminutive man, though a bit pudgy. Apparently he'd put on a good deal of weight since his marriage, whenever that was, because his wedding ring seemed to be strangling his finger. He had a pleasant round face, ruddy cheeks, and brown hair that was receding back over the top of his head. He wore square tortoiseshell glasses and was fond of sweaters and chinos. The front of his desk was pushed against the wall of his office so he could sit with students without anything between them.

When Pamela entered his office the next day, she thought she had a lot to say; once she'd seated herself, however, she couldn't remember what and just sat there fidgeting for a while.

"Did you enjoy Mr. Lehman's classes?" Mr. Elliot asked,

smiling slightly. He was leaning back in his chair, his left elbow resting on the desk top and his hand propping up his head.

"Oh, very *much*," Pamela said enthusiastically. "He was funny and interesting. I've never enjoyed English so much before. And he never made any of us feel like we were just . . . students. Do you know what I mean?"

He nodded. "I think so."

"He treated us the same way he would treat anyone else, young or old. He . . . *liked* us. I think, anyway. I had his class right after lunch, and lunch, you know, is a period where you can kind of relax . . . lay back. Well, those of us who had him right after lunch had *two* periods where we could relax. Not that he didn't make us work, because he did. But it was work we enjoyed. I think because he made us all feel like we could do it, no matter what it was."

They talked for a while about Mr. Lehman, about how Pamela felt now that he was gone. She talked a little, cried a little, then talked some more. Once she felt better and had dried her eyes and blown her nose, Mr. Elliot started to stand to escort her out, but she remained seated.

"There was something else I wanted to talk to you about," she said.

His eyebrows rose, and he adjusted his glasses as he took his seat again. "Sure, Pamela. What is it?"

"Do you know Lenny Cochran?"

Mr. Elliot leaned his head back, squinting slightly. "Yes. A thin boy? With glasses? Yes, I know who Lenny is, why?"

"Well, maybe I'm out of line here, but he's a good friend of mine and . . . I'm worried about him." Slowly, hesitantly, she told him first about Lenny's problems at home with his alcoholic father, then about his elaborate, bizarre fantasy involving Mr. Trancas. When she was finished, she sighed and bowed her head, feeling ashamed, as if she had betrayed her friend.

Mr. Elliot leaned forward in his chair, frowning. He was silent for a long time, scratching his cheek absently, chewing on his lower lip. Finally, he asked, "And you think Lenny really believes this? About Mr. Trancas?"

"Well . . . I'm not sure. He *seems* to, but he's pretty good at that. This doesn't seem like a joke, though. He seems really *upset* about it, and I think he *does* believe it. But I think maybe . . . well, I guess this is your department, and I probably don't know what I'm talking about, but I think it's got something to do with his dad and what's going on at home. Maybe he's looking for attention or maybe he's just . . . I don't know, upset enough to believe this sort of thing. Whatever it is, it's really bothering him. He's . . . *different*. And I'm worried. Maybe I shouldn't be talking about him like this, but—"

"No, no, Pamela. You did the right thing. I'm just not sure what I should do. Do you mind if I ask you a few questions about Lenny?"

"Sure. Go ahead."

And he did. He asked about Lenny's likes and dislikes, his hobbies. Writing? What kind of writing? What was his general attitude, his overall mood? Had his mood changed suddenly?

She answered all of his questions, and when they were through, she said, "Mr. Elliot, I hope you won't tell Lenny that I came to you about this. I don't think he'd be too happy."

"Don't worry," he said, smiling as he took her elbow in a gentlemanly fashion and led her to the door. "I'll just talk with him and see what I can come up with. But I'm glad you came to me. Don't feel bad about this. You *should* be concerned about your friends."

She thanked him and left his office. But as she walked down the hall she felt uneasy. If Lenny suspected her, if he thought she had told his story to Mr. Elliot, he would not be happy. And she valued Lenny's friendship too much to lose it over such a thing.

Then again, maybe she *had* done the right thing. Maybe Mr. Elliot would approach the subject in a subtle way, so Lenny wouldn't suspect anything. Maybe he'd do it so subtly that Lenny wouldn't realize it was being approached at all. And maybe talking about it would ease Lenny's mind and make him better.

She didn't care *how* it happened, she just wanted things to be the way they were before.

Of course, that would never happen. Things would never be the same again, now that Mr. Lehman was gone for good.

"I thought we were supposed to just drop in," Lenny said, trying to look and sound casual as he took a seat in Mr. Elliot's office. He hoped his smile and pleasant, alert tone of voice would hide his exhaustion and anxiety. When he'd gotten the call over the P.A. in class to go to Mr. Elliot's office, he'd immediately become afraid. He wasn't sure why . . . but then, he wasn't thinking too well these days; there was too much that he knew *should* frighten him.

"Is this a problem?" Mr. Elliot asked nicely. "I didn't mean to interrupt—"

"On, no," Lenny said quickly, "I'm not complaining. You got me out of history class."

They both laughed quietly.

Mr. Elliot leaned back in his chair, crossed his legs, and said, "It's just that so many of the students have come in already. To talk about Mr. Lehman's, uh . . . unfortunate fate. It's hit all of us pretty hard. Plus . . ." Mr. Elliot sucked his teeth noisily, thoughtfully. "Your friends are a bit concerned about you."

Lenny held his breath a second, then tried to relax, not wanting *anything* to show.

"They haven't seen much of you lately and . . . well, they thought that perhaps the recent . . . tragedy had had a particular effect on you."

Lenny thought a moment about what to say next. "What friends? I mean, have people been . . . *complaining* about me?"

Mr. Elliot chuckled. "Nothing like that, Lenny. And, of course, my job as a counselor does not allow me to repeat conversations I have with students or hand out names indiscriminately, but . . . I would think you would be pleased to know there are people concerned about you."

"Well . . . yeah. I guess so."

"Look, Lenny, it's okay if Mr. Lehman's death has hit you hard. Some students haven't even come back to school. That doesn't mean it's hit them any harder. It just means that they're handling it differently. And everyone . . . *ev-eryone* handles things like this differently. For example, when you go to a horror movie, have you ever noticed that, during the really scary parts, some people *laugh*? I mean, they laugh like it's a comedy! Now, to some people, that's strange; some people think that means they're insensitive or that they *enjoy* the kind of thing that's happening on screen. But it's just their way of handling it. Some people will simply get up and walk out, while others just sit stiffly in their seats, like mannequins. And others will actually cry. You see, everybody processes things differently. So, no matter what you're feeling—depressed, angry, let down—you shouldn't be ashamed of it. And it'll feel a lot better if you talk about it."

Good speech, Lenny thought. *Gee, I wonder what he'd think if I told him that what I'm feeling is* afraid *because I think my English teacher is planning to torture and kill a good friend of mine . . . and maybe me too?* But instead, he said, "Well . . . I guess I'm feeling all of those things."

"Were you close to Mr. Lehman?"

"I wouldn't say *close*, but he was my favorite teacher." He kept his voice even and fought to control his face.

"So he was . . . important to you?"

"Of course."

"You looked up to him? Respected him?"

"Yes." Lenny was growing impatient and fidgety, but he tried not to show it.

"Well . . . that's a kind of closeness, don't you think? *I'd* say you were close to him."

"Okay, okay, if you want to put it that way."

"So, what do you think of Mr. Trancas?"

Lenny stared at his lap and prayed for the strength to hold in his reaction. He stared at his lap for a long time.

"Lenny?"

"Hm?"

"What do you think of Mr. Trancas? Your new English teacher?"

It's showing, he thought. *He knows something's wrong.*

Lenny looked at Mr. Elliot and smiled. "He's fine. I mean, you know . . . it's just been a few days, but . . . yeah, he seems fine to me."

"You're comfortable with him, then?"

Lenny felt a peculiar tickling sensation on his forehead. Was that sweat breaking out on his forehead?

"Comfortable?" Lenny asked, and his voice broke ever so slightly. "What exactly do you mean by comfortable?"

"I mean, do you feel all right having him as your teacher? Do you think you could have the same kind of relationship with him that you had with Mr. Lehman?"

What Lenny really wanted to say was, *No, I don't think so, because I found Mr. Lehman's corpse in Mr. Trancas's woodshed, so I don't think I'm ever going to have what you could call a really healthy teacher-student relationship with the guy.* But he knew Mr. Elliot wouldn't believe him. He'd probably think Lenny was crazy, and he might contact Lenny's parents which would just make things at home even worse.

Lenny said, "Well, like I told you before, it hasn't been very long."

"Then you're not sure."

"*Sure?* Um . . ." Lenny swallowed hard. He was getting *very* uncomfortable. "Look, is this some kind of interrogation? I mean, I feel like I'm being questioned downtown at the police station, you know what I mean?" He slipped his thumb and forefinger under his glasses and wiped the sweat from the bridge of his nose, then stood and walked around his chair. Standing behind it, he put his hands on its back, leaned forward, and said, "Listen, Mr. Elliot, I'm a little uncomfortable with this, okay? I can't believe you've been doing this with everyone who's come in here today, and I'm kind of wondering why you're doing it to *me*? What am I, some kind of suspect? Do you think I've *done* something? Is there anything you haven't told me? Huh?"

Mr. Elliot shifted in his chair. "I'm sorry, Lenny, I didn't mean to upset you. Please sit down."

Lenny didn't sit. Actually, he *couldn't* because his knees were shivering too much to walk back around the chair. So he remained where he stood, leaning over the chair, looking at Mr. Elliot expectantly.

The counselor leaned forward, straightened his glasses, and said, "Lenny, there have been a lot of students through here today and no two of them have been alike. Everyone reacts differently to something like this, and I never know *how* a student is going to react, so I have to ask questions. Whatever questions come to mind. Whatever questions seem appropriate. Please . . . sit down."

Taking a deep breath to steady himself, Lenny moved around the chair, and sat down, trying not to *look* like he was avoiding Mr. Elliot's eyes, although that was exactly what he was doing. "Okay," he whispered. "I'm sitting."

They talked for a while after that and things seemed to settle down. Mr. Elliot's questions from then on were very casual, bland, as if he'd finally realized that Lenny had been uncomfortable with his questions before. When they were done—at least, when Lenny *thought* they were done—he stood and smiled.

"Well," he said, "I should get to my next class."

Mr. Elliot stood, too, nodding. "Okay, Lenny. It's been a pleasure talking with you. I hope you'll come in again soon. On your own, I mean. You're always welcome, you know. I've enjoyed this, and I'd like to do it again."

"Yeah. Maybe. Uh . . . thanks for getting me out of history class."

"Anytime."

When he left Mr. Elliot's office, Lenny was afraid the entire school could hear his sigh of relief.

Mr. Elliot sat back down in his chair, turned to his desk, and sighed. It was obvious that there really *was* something to what Pamela had told him. Lenny clearly had a problem with Mr. Trancas. Perhaps it stemmed from Lenny's problems at home, perhaps it was something much deeper. Then again, it might be just a clash of personalities.

Before he made a judgment, Mr. Elliot thought it might be a good idea for him to have a word with Mr. Trancas. Perhaps then he would be able to get a better handle on the situation.

Yes, he thought, nodding to himself, *I'll talk with Mr. Trancas. Casually. See what he has to say.*

Nodding again, he made a mental note to go see Mr. Trancas sometime that day.

Mr. Elliot waited outside the door to Mr. Trancas's classroom until the last bell of the day rang. He smiled at the students as they rushed out; most of them didn't notice him and just hurried down the hall. When they were all gone, he stepped into the room and saw Mr. Trancas behind his desk, apparently absorbed in a stack of papers before him.

"Mr. Trancas?"

He looked up and smiled haltingly.

Mr. Elliot closed the door and walked in smiling. "Mr. Trancas. I hope I'm not coming in at a bad time."

"Not at all." Mr. Trancas stood, looking a bit curious. "What can I do for you?"

"Well . . . do you have a few minutes?"

"Sure."

Mr. Elliot pulled one of the school desks over and seated himself beside Mr. Trancas, facing him. "Actually, you can't *do* anything for me. I was just curious to see how things are going. I know how it is to be a new faculty member. I started right in the middle of a school year myself. It's kind of uncomfortable. Takes some adjustment. I just wanted to see how things were going."

Without losing his smile, Mr. Trancas said, "You think I need some therapy because I'm *new*?"

Mr. Elliot tried not to flinch or look too surprised. He thought that was a rather strange reaction, a bit too defensive. But he tried not to skip a beat and said, "Of course not. I just thought you might like to talk."

"Oh. Well." Mr. Trancas leaned back in his chair, locked his hands behind his head, and crossed his legs. "I think so far things are going pretty well. Actually, I'm very glad I'm here. I just wish I could have come under different . . . more positive circumstances."

"Well, I'm glad to hear that. You're getting along with the students all right?"

"Perfectly."

Mr. Trancas seemed to be waiting for something. He looked at Mr. Elliot as if he were expecting him to say something else: eyes narrowed, one brow cocked questioningly. Mr. Elliot felt he should get on with his questions right away—he *was* planning to work up to them subtly—but he wasn't sure exactly how to ask them, or how Mr.

Trancas would take them. He certainly didn't want to arouse Mr. Trancas's suspicion.

"If you don't mind my asking, how are you getting along with Lenny Cochran?"

"Lenny? Well . . . no, I don't mind, but why are you asking?"

"Lenny has been seeing me. He has some . . . well, some problems. I'm just curious. How is he doing in your class?"

"Very well, actually. He's a bright boy. In fact, he seems to be quite a good writer. Of course—" He chuckled. "—his interest lies in areas of which I don't approve. He wants to be a *horror* writer. Why he would want to waste his talent on such a nasty genre, I don't know, but he *is* talented."

Mr. Elliot nodded, trying to form his next question. "Have you had a chance to talk with him?"

"Not really. We've spoken briefly, but that's all."

"He seems to be doing well."

"Oh, definitely."

"And . . . you get along okay?"

"Of course. Why *wouldn't* we get along?" Mr. Trancas frowned slightly, looking puzzled.

Mr. Elliot held up a hand and shook his head. "Just asking. Lenny's been having some problems, and I was just wondering if perhaps you'd . . . noticed anything."

"No, I haven't noticed a thing. He seems perfectly healthy to me . . . mentally and physically. Is it anything serious?"

"No, no. I don't think it's *too* serious. I suspect it's connected to some problems he's having at home. Things don't seem to be going too well there."

"Sorry to hear that."

Mr. Elliot realized he wasn't going to get anything more, so he stood and said good-bye. As he walked down the hall he wondered how much truth there was to Pamela's story. Could Lenny actually think Mr. Trancas was some kind of psychopath? If so, then Lenny had some serious problems. Perhaps things were worse for him at home than Mr. Elliot had thought.

Back in the classroom, Mr. Trancas sat behind his desk staring out the window. He was perfectly still except for one finger that kept dragging its nail over the desk top with a hiss. The room was silent except for the slight crunching coming from Mr. Trancas's mouth as he ground his teeth together. Watching through the window, his eyes followed Lenny as he walked with Pamela away from the building and toward the parking lot.

"That boy has become a problem," Mr. Trancas whispered to himself.

He sat that way for a long time, even after Lenny had gone out of sight . . . just staring out the window, scraping his nail, and grinding his teeth. . . .

FOURTEEN

ABDUCTION!

"Did you say something to Mr. Elliot about me today?" Lenny asked Pamela as they walked to the parking lot.

"Why?"

"Just answer." He didn't mean to snap at her, but his voice was abrupt, and he apologized. "Sorry, I'm just . . . I don't know."

"I wish you did, because *I* sure don't know what's wrong with you." She stopped and faced him. "You haven't been acting yourself lately, Lenny. I was worried, that's all. So I . . . I mentioned it to Mr. Elliot. That's all."

"*What* did you mention to Mr. Elliot?"

"Well, I told him you've been getting some . . . you know, some strange ideas. Like, about . . . Mr. Trancas." She looked away guiltily, then sighed. "Look, if you're mad at me, I'm sorry. I was just concerned, is all. Want a ride home?"

"So *that* was why he kept asking questions about Trancas," Lenny muttered. "No, Pamela, I'm not mad at you. I just wish you weren't quite so concerned."

"Well, I wouldn't be if you'd just tell me what's wrong."

He shook his head slowly as they walked to Pamela's car. "You wouldn't believe me."

"Why?"

"Because you haven't up to now, and because I don't have any proof of it."

"What? Are you *still* on that story about Mr. Trancas?"

"See what I mean? You don't believe me. Not now, anyway. But I'll tell you something, Pamela," he said as they got into the car. Turning to her, he said quietly, "If anything happens to me, you'll know I've been telling the truth."

She looked at him for a long time, lips parted, eyes a little wide, as if his words had struck her hard. For a moment, she seemed about to speak, perhaps to ask for an explanation. But instead, she started the car and drove out of the parking lot.

After dinner that night, Lenny went to his room and started on some homework.

It wasn't long before the shouting began. He heard his father cursing as he stalked down the hall and into the other bedroom. "I *told* you it was right here!" he shouted.

His mom said something, her voice quiet.

"I can *see* it's not there now! Lenny! Leonard! Come here—now!"

Sick with dread, Lenny went into the hallway and looked into his parents' bedroom.

"Have you seen the camera?" his father barked.

Lenny's first reaction was to lie and say he hadn't seen the camera just to avoid being yelled at for a while and maybe even swatted around a little. But he knew that wouldn't work because his father wouldn't believe him, and he'd just yell at him and probably rough him up anyway, so Lenny told the truth.

"I'm sorry," he said. "I . . . borrowed it last night. To take a few pictures. And it got . . . lost."

There was a moment of silence, then an angry storm from his father. "Borrowed? You *borrowed* it then *lost* it? You know how much that camera cost me? I'm not made of money, you know. Who told you you could borrow the camera, anyway? I need it tomorrow to take some pictures at the store. You have no right taking our things . . ."

The ranting went on and on.

Lenny stepped back suddenly as his father swept his arm over the top of a small hallway table and knocked a vase of silk flowers and an ashtray to the floor. Both of them shattered. Then he kicked the table over, shouting at Lenny the whole time, arms flailing until . . .

. . . he slapped Lenny's face. Then again. Lenny slammed back against the wall and slid to the floor, shielding his face with his arms. But he wasn't there long. His father clutched the front of his shirt and lifted him to his feet, leaning so close that Lenny could smell the reek of whiskey on his breath.

"You're going to buy a brand-new camera, do you understand, boy?" he bellowed into Lenny's face, pressing him hard against the wall. "And you're going to pay for every damned cent of it yourself! No loans, no credit, no ***nothin'***! And I don't care how you do it! Do you understand me?"

Lenny nodded, but his head hurt. He could feel his cheek sting and knew it must be bright red.

"And if you ever—and I mean *ever*—touch any of our stuff again, I'll beat you so long and so hard, you'll pray to see your maker, is that clear, boy?"

Lenny took too long to nod his reply, and his father tightened his grip on Lenny's shirt.

"I said, is that *clear*?"

Lenny nodded.

His father backed away but didn't stop shouting at him, calling him names, insulting him, cursing him.

Lenny nodded at the appropriate times as he turned and went back into his bedroom. The shouting continued as he closed and locked his bedroom door.

"Don't you close the door on me, boy! You hear me? Open this damned door!"

Then his mother got into it. That was the order of things; he'd yell at Mom for a while, then at Lenny, maybe rough him up, then Mom would stand up for Lenny, and he would lay into her then. It was the same thing every time.

Lenny turned on the radio, hoping to drown out the sound of his father's voice, his slurred words and drunken anger. He tried to tell himself, as he had for so many years, that it was the alcohol. He knew his father could be a nice guy now and then because he'd *seen* it; but it was only now and then . . . because of the alcohol. Somehow, that didn't make it any easier to take. If it was so obvious to Lenny, surely it was obvious to his father. So why would he want to drink something that made him behave that way, *feel* that way? Why didn't he *quit*?

"More stormy weather on the way, kids," the disc jockey said cheerfully. "So stay out of that rain and stay *close* to your radio . . . close and *intimate* . . . with Heart . . ."

As Heart's newest song began the telephone rang, and Lenny jumped. He picked it up and said hello.

"What're you up to?" Pamela asked.

"Um . . . well . . ."

"And don't go whining to your friends about how mean your old man is!" his father roared on the other side of the door, pounding it a couple times. "You're lucky I don't rip out your stereo and *sell* it to pay for the camera, you lousy thief!"

Pamela was quiet for a long moment, then said, "Uh, this sounds like maybe a bad time?"

"Yeah. Kinda."

"You want me to call back? Or better yet, why don't we go out? We can have a Coke over at the Burger Barrel, huh?"

"Well, I don't know if—"

"Are you listening to me, boy?" his father shouted, pounding the door again. Mom said something to him, but he shouted at her too. "You just stay out of this!"

"Oh, Lenny," Pamela whispered, "I'm so sorry. Are you sure you don't want to come with me? Please? We don't really have to *do* anything. You just need to get out of there, I think."

Lenny thought about it. She was right, he needed to get out of the house, but he wasn't in the mood for anyone's company.

"Not now," he said. "But thanks. And I'll call you before I go to bed. I promise. But I've gotta go now, really, so . . . thanks for calling, and I'll talk to you later." He hung up quickly, without even waiting for her good-bye, because he just couldn't take it anymore . . . the shouting, the pounding.

He put on his jacket and crawled out his window, leaving his father's voice behind.

Lenny walked through the cold misty night with his hands stuffed into his jacket pockets, feeling depressed, but trying not to let that feeling stick. The feeling that was even harder to deal with was his fear.

What would Mr. Trancas do now that he had those pictures from the camera? Assuming, of course, that those snapshots *were* the pictures from the camera. Why would Mr. Trancas have behaved that way in class if they were anything else? Mr. Trancas knew . . . of course he knew. But he also knew, no doubt, that there was no way Lenny could prove what *he* knew, so maybe he wouldn't try anything. Then again, how could one predict the actions of a lunatic? A lunatic who had killed . . . well, God only knew *how* many people he'd killed.

Lenny walked for blocks and blocks, paying little attention to where he was or what direction he was going in, staring mostly at his feet as they slapped the wet sidewalk.

Cars drove by now and then, their tires hissing over the wet pavement. He hardly noticed them. One of them even slowed to a stop and parked at the curb behind him. He only vaguely heard the engine die, the door open and slam shut, the footsteps that followed. In fact, he completely ignored the footsteps, so he didn't notice that they were following him, moving faster and faster, closing in on him. He was lost in his own thoughts until a familiar voice said, "Lenny?"

He stopped and spun around, facing the man behind him. "Mr. Tranc—"

Mr. Trancas slapped a cloth over his face that smelled awful, but the smell didn't last long because Lenny found himself sliding down into blackness . . . into unconsciousness . . . until there was nothing.

FIFTEEN

IN THE BASEMENT

When Lenny awoke, he was lying on his back staring at a maze of pipes through dim, hazy light. His head ached, his mouth was dry, and there was a horrible smell in his nostrils. When he started to sit up, a voice said, "Hello, Lenny."

He turned to see Mr. Trancas seated beside him in a folding canvas chair. Smiling.

"How do you feel?" Mr. Trancas asked. "Do you have a headache?"

Confused, Lenny frowned and nodded.

"Well, that's to be expected. It's from the ether."

"Ether?"

"Mm-hm. It was on the cloth that I put over your face.

Sometimes it leaves you with a headache. It'll pass. If you'd like, I can give you some aspirin."

Lenny nodded and Mr. Trancas left for a moment, then came back with two aspirins and a glass of water, smiling. Lenny swallowed the caplets and handed the glass back to Mr. Trancas, wincing with each small movement.

Mr. Trancas put the glass on a nightstand. The nightstand was very familiar. It wasn't until that moment that Lenny realized where he was.

He was in Mr. Trancas's basement, lying on the cot.

"You're probably wondering what you're doing here," Mr. Trancas said, still smiling. "The ether tends to leave you a little confused."

Lenny nodded.

"Well, I was out driving. Just to relax, actually, because I've got a lot on my mind at the moment. And I saw you walking. Well, I thought to myself, he knows more about me than I *want* him to know, but he doesn't know enough about me to know that I'm not the psychopath he probably *thinks* I am, so what should I do?" He shrugged, then slapped his hands on his thighs and leaned forward, grinning. "Well, I thought the best thing to do would be to bring you home."

His voice thick, his throat sore, Lenny asked hoarsely, "And you just happened to have some ether in your car?"

"Yes, as a matter of fact, I did." He looked very happy with himself. "I decided that the best thing would be to bring you home and show you that what I do is not as psychopathic as you probably think. Oh, by the way. The pictures were very nice. Not the ones you took *here*. I mean the ones of your family. The Christmas pictures. All of you gathered around the tree. Unwrapping your presents. Yes, they were very nice. In fact, I've often wished that *I* had time for a family. A wife . . . children . . . a dog . . . with all the trimmings . . . you know, the tree at Christmas time, the turkey on Thanksgiving. But there's simply too much work to be done. I mean the kind of work I've been doing for years now. The kind of work that you have apparently mistaken for insanity."

Lenny was too weary and in too much pain to be very frightened. So, he simply asked, "And what kind of . . . of work is that?"

"Teaching. Oh, not the teaching *you're* familiar with in the American school system. I mean *real* teaching. The teaching of truly important subjects, taught in a way that will *work*. Education these days . . . well, it is sorely lacking in impact. That's obvious by the statistics. I mean, look at how many people watch television and how few read books. Look at how many people want to depend on their dishonesty, their chicanery, rather than depend on their skill and intelligence. The country is in terrible shape, Lenny. Lazy and fat and spoiled. I know, because I've been all over it, looking for . . . well, for the *perfect* students. The ones who *want* to learn, the ones who *enjoy* knowledge. They're rare, but they're out there. And *I* find them, Lenny. They don't always succeed . . . but I do find them."

"Is . . . is that why I'm here?"

"No . . . not exactly. You're here because you got in the way. I originally intended to tutor another student . . . well, *you* know who I had in mind. Your friend Pamela. But, I've been thinking about it, and actually, I'm glad you're here. You seem to have some potential. You seem to enjoy learning. And you certainly have a talent for writing. In fact, I think you have the *gift* of writing. You're simply . . . misguided. That's all."

Lenny frowned.

"Yes, misguided. I mean . . . *Fangoria*? Horror? Surely you don't actually want to write horror. Do you? It's so . . . distasteful. It has no purpose or value. And that, my boy, is where I come in. I am going to teach you things with purpose and value, great value. And when I'm through with you—" He stood, towering over the cot. "—*if* you listen and follow the rules and work hard, that is—you will be a new person. You will look at your whole life differently." He just stood there and looked at Lenny for a while, then said, "But now you need some rest. I'll come down and check on you after a while." He turned, headed up the stairs, and out of the basement, closing the door softly behind him. The clicking sound of the lock seemed to echo in the basement.

Lenny's eyes moved to the school desk in the middle of the room and the manacles hanging over it, and his stomach turned slowly inside.

SIXTEEN

AN EMPTY SEAT

"I don't think there's anything to worry about," David said to Pamela over lunch. "He probably just decided to stay home. If his dad was as angry as you say he sounded, then he might've given Lenny a shiner."

"But I tried calling him and got no answer," Pamela said.

"Look, he was probably sleeping, or lying down with an ice bag on his face," Todd said. "He'll be back tomorrow."

"How can you guys talk so casually about something so horrible?" Pamela asked, sitting beside the empty seat that was usually occupied by Lenny. "How would you like it if *your* fathers treated *you* that way, huh?"

"We've known him since we were kids, Pamela," David

said. "Yes, it's horrible, the way his dad treats him, but we've come to . . . well, to sort of live with it. The way he has. That doesn't mean we're happy about it."

Charlene and Teresa had been silent up until then.

"Why don't we go see him after school?" Teresa asked.

"Yeah," Todd agreed. "Good idea. We'll drop in on him after school and take him out. Have a burger, or something. He'll be fine. He's been putting up with it for a long time now."

But somehow, Pamela's worries did not go away. What if there was more to his absence than his argument with his father last night?

"Boy," David said, chuckling, "you're sure awfully worried about him, aren't you?" He winked. "Is there maybe something a little more than just a friendship going on here?"

"Oh, knock it off." She sighed, annoyed. "I'm just concerned. That's all."

"Well, don't worry," Todd assured her. "We'll see him after school."

As they pulled up to Lenny's house in David's car, Pamela's blood ran cold. She was sitting beside Teresa in the front seat and stiffened, clutching Teresa's arm suddenly as she gasped, "The police."

A police car was parked in front of the house.

Somehow, it fit. Even though the sight of the police car shocked her, Pamela thought it seemed to fit with the feeling of dread that had been dogging her all day. Apparently, her feeling had been right; there *was* more to Lenny's absence than his argument with his father.

They'd parked the car and were on their way up the

front walk when the front door swung open and Mrs. Cochran slammed through the screen door and rushed down the steps toward them. Her eyes were wide and sticky with tears, and she held her arms out before her as if she were groping for them. She came straight to Pamela, gripped her shoulders and asked in a trembling, frantic whisper, "Have you seen him? Please? Have you seen Lenny today?"

Mrs. Cochran's panic hit Pamela hard, and she felt tears welling in her eyes. "No, we haven't," she said.

"I thought he'd gotten up early, was all. I figured he'd just jumped out of bed and left the house. He's done it before. But then the school called. They wanted to know why he hadn't come in today, and . . . I got scared. I called Phil, my husband, at work, and he hasn't seen him, either. And I-I-I just didn't know what to—"

"Why don't you kids come on inside," a voice said, and Pamela looked up to see Mr. Cochran on the porch, holding the door open.

Pamela put her arm around Mrs. Cochran's waist, and the six of them went into the house. Officer Jerry Gideon was seated on the sofa, leaning forward with his elbows on his knees, holding a notepad in his hand. He greeted them with a solemn nod, then looked up at Mrs. Cochran with concern.

"I understand how you feel, Mrs. Cochran," he said, "but you've gotta believe me when I tell you this happens a lot. Kids do it all the time, get pissed off—em, s'cuse me—they get angry with their parents, have an argument, or whatever, and they just take off. But they almost always come back with their tails between their legs, I promise."

"How can you *say* that?" Mrs. Cochran asked breathlessly. "You aren't *sure*. You don't *know*."

"No, I don't know. But he hasn't been gone that long, and I've seen this happen so many times that I'll bet you my next paycheck he'll be home before bedtime tonight. Maybe before dinner. Don't worry, though, I'll put out the word and have everybody keep their eyes open." He turned to Pamela and the others then, and asked, "Would you kids have any idea where Lenny might've gone?"

They all responded immediately with shakes of their heads and quiet nos and uh-uhs .. all but Pamela.

If anything happens to me, you'll know I've been telling the truth, Lenny had said. She considered sharing that with Officer Gideon, but then she would have to tell him the whole story. What would he think of it? He'd probably think she and Lenny were *both* crazy! Then he'd probably stick to his idea that Lenny had just run away for a little while and would be back sooner than they all thought.

So, finally, Pamela simply shook her head like the others and said she had no idea where Lenny might have gone.

"Well," Officer Gideon said, "give him a little time. That's probably all he wanted, really: a little time alone. He'll no doubt be back soon enough. But in the meantime, we'll be on the lookout for him. In fact, you know what else I'll do?"

Everyone in the room watched Officer Gideon expectantly as he looked thoughtfully at Mrs. Cochran.

"There's word out about a stranger who's been hanging around town," he said. "A tall man with an eyepatch. I've heard he's been seen a few times hanging around the school. I'll try to look him up, ask him a few questions.

Would that make you feel better? I mean, after all, he's probably the most suspicious person in town, right?"

Mrs. Cochran chewed on a knuckle and nodded half-heartedly.

It was painfully obvious to Pamela that Officer Gideon was being condescending toward the Cochrans, but, of course, she said nothing.

Officer Gideon closed his notepad and slipped it in his pocket, then took his cap from the sofa and put it on. "Call the station if you hear from Lenny. And I'll call you, of course, if anything comes up." He said good-bye to everyone, then left Mr. and Mrs. Cochran, Pamela, and the others in the room, standing in uncomfortable silence.

Finally, Mr. Cochran—who somehow looked older than usual this afternoon, a little stooped and droopy—stepped toward his wife and put a hand on her shoulder. "If you want," he said softly, "we can go out and drive around. Look for him."

"I don't know," she replied, her thick, emotional voice laced with sarcasm. "Should you be driving? Or have you been drinking all day in the back room of the hardware store?"

Pamela was embarrassed suddenly, but obviously not as embarrassed as Mr. Cochran. His eyes darted past them, and he bowed his head, turning away.

"No, I . . . I haven't been . . . drinking. Shall I get the keys?"

"I don't know," she replied. "Do you think he'd even come near us if he saw you in the car? He might never get in with you. I certainly wouldn't. Who wants to get yelled at and hit some more?"

Mr. Cochran took in a deep breath, and his shoulders sagged slowly as he exhaled. "Shall I get the keys?"

"Oh, all right."

"Would you like us to ride around and look too?" David asked. "I've got my car."

Mrs. Cochran tried to smile at him, but failed. "Would you mind?"

Pamela took her hand. "No, Mrs. Cochran, we wouldn't mind at all."

On the front walk, on their way back to the car, Todd said quietly, "Jeez, I've never seen Mrs. Cochran stand up to him that way before."

"Me, either," David agreed, shocked.

"Well, it seemed to work, huh?" Charlene asked.

"Probably because he's ashamed of himself," Teresa said with a little satisfaction. "And he should be."

But Pamela added nothing to the conversation. The more she thought about what Lenny had said, the more she began to think that maybe—just *maybe*—Mr. Cochran had nothing to do with Lenny's disappearance.

SEVENTEEN

SCHOOL TIME, SCHOOL TIME HAPPY GOLDEN RULE TIME

No matter what time of day it was, the light in the basement remained the same: dim and shadowy. The air was damp and chilly, and under different circumstances, Lenny would have been very uncomfortable, but Mr. Trancas had provided him with several blankets, and besides that, Lenny's fear and anxiety did a lot to keep him warm, even a bit sweaty.

That morning—Lenny wasn't sure exactly at what time because he didn't have a watch or clock—Mr. Trancas awakened him and gave him a breakfast tray of eggs, bacon, toast, and orange juice, then put a stack of books on his nightstand.

"I have to go to work now," he said, "but I'd like you to read your assignments in these books."

"Assignments?" Lenny asked in a hoarse voice.

"Yes, they're written in here." From the bottom of the stack, Mr. Trancas removed a thick three-ring binder, opened it, and leaned forward to show Lenny a page of assignments he'd written. "As you can see, there is a reading assignment—James Joyce, which is in the stack, here—and a writing assignment covering specific points of what you've read, then an English assignment dealing with grammar, a geography assignment, and a couple of chemistry assignments. All the reading material you need is right here. In this pocket of the binder there are plenty of pens and pencils and erasers. Of *course* I expect your penmanship to be at its best and your papers to be very neat." He stood, closed the binder, and put it on top of the stack. "When I get home, we'll talk about all you've done, you can take a break, then we'll do some more. After I've looked over your papers, of course. And at the end of the day there will be a test. There will *always* be a test at the end of the day, so keep that in mind. Any questions?"

Still only half awake and a little confused, Lenny shook his head and said, "No. No questions."

Mr. Trancas leaned over, took a small brown bag from the floor, and put it on top of the stack of books. "I've packed a school lunch for you," he said, rather happily. "It should hold you until I get home and fix you a hot dinner. Of course, you'll want to get to bed rather early tonight. I won't be getting you up this late tomorrow. Your days will begin early so we can work for a few hours together before I go to the school. Sound good?" he asked, clapping his hands together, then rubbing his palms enthusiastically.

No, Lenny wanted to say, *it sounds like my worst nightmare, like a living hell.*

Instead, he nodded, because he knew to do anything else would be pointless.

"All right. In that case, Leonard, I'll be on my way, and you can get to your studies." Mr. Trancas did a very strange thing then. He gave Lenny a very formal, polite half-bow, leaning forward with his hands folded before him.

And then he left.

Lenny spent the rest of the day doing his assignments. They were not difficult, not like assignments he got in school that took a little while to do. These assignments were *hard*. They took a long time. They looked, to Lenny, like college assignments. He had no idea why Mr. Trancas was giving them to him. He had to be insane.

Of course he's insane, Lenny thought. *A teacher doesn't lock a student up in a basement with cables and manacles unless he's* insane!

But, hard as they were and although it took all day, he did finish the assignments. His only fear was that he hadn't done them correctly.

What would happen then? How would he be punished? He wasn't sure, but he had a good idea that those manacles had something to do with it, and however they were involved, they scared him to death, and he wanted nothing to do with them.

Lenny lay back on his cot and covered his eyes with his forearms. After a while, he actually began to relax, and for a moment, he thought he might drift off for a nap of blissful sleep.

Of course, he hadn't spent the entire day on *just* his assignments. He'd spent a good deal of time running around the basement trying to find a way out. He'd pounded on the door at the top of the stairs, screaming at the top of his lungs; he'd done the same with the boards that had been nailed over the basement window that was visible outside in the front yard.

But afterward, after he'd waited some time for some kind of response—a voice, a single sound from outside, *anything*—he realized that it was useless. He was trapped. No one knew he was there. No one would—or *could*—hear him or see him, and he was completely cut off from the outside. All he had were his assignments.

Then, after lying on the cot for a while with his arm over his eyes, he heard a car pull into the driveway.

Lenny sat up immediately.

He heard the engine stop, heard the car door open and close, heard Mr. Trancas's footsteps, heard him enter the front door and walk through the house whistling.

It was a while—maybe twenty minutes or so, Lenny guessed—before Mr. Trancas came down into the basement. When he did, he wore a sweatshirt and jeans and was smiling.

"Hello, Lenny. Hungry?"

"Yeah, as a matter of fact, I am."

"Well, dinner is cooking. Did you do all of your assignments?"

"Uh-huh." Lenny's voice sounded small; he was too frightened and filled with dread to be very friendly or very enthusiastic.

"Good, very good. Tell you what. You give me your

papers, I'll go up and start reading them, and when your dinner is ready, I'll bring it down."

Sitting on the side of the cot, Lenny found it very hard to smile, but he did his best as he handed up to Mr. Trancas the three-ring binder in which he'd done his work.

"Great," Mr. Trancas said. "How does Salisbury steak with mashed potatoes and gravy and some mixed vegetables and a hot dinner roll sound? With a little strawberry ice cream for dessert?"

"Fine," Lenny said without enthusiasm.

"Good. I'll be back in a while." He turned and left the basement.

Lenny lay back down on the cot, wishing he could sleep; he was only able to wait, fidgeting nervously and filled with dread.

Officer Gideon spotted the eyepatched stranger quite unexpectedly as he was driving back to the station that evening to finish up the end of his shift. He knew that his new wife was waiting with a late dinner, and he was looking forward not only to eating but to being with her. But when he saw the man walking down the opposite side of the street—the eyepatch made him stand out immediately—Gideon figured it wouldn't hurt to stop and have a word with him. After all, he'd promised the Cochrans he would.

"Excuse me," he said through his window, stopping the car. "You want to wait right there while I park the car?"

"Certainly," the man said politely. He stood on the sidewalk with his hands buried in the pockets of his dark overcoat, watching Officer Gideon park the patrol car.

"Hi, there," Gideon said, getting out of the car and

slamming the door. He smiled, not wanting to put the man on the defensive. "How are you this evening?"

"Just fine, officer. How are you?"

"Oh, I can't complain. Sorry to bother you, but I saw you walking down the street and thought I'd stop and have a word."

"Is anything wrong?"

"Well . . ." Officer Gideon hooked his thumbs in his back pockets and looked the man over, taking in what little he could see of the stranger's face. "Do you live around here?"

"Oh, no," the man said, smiling. "I'm from out of town. I live in southern California."

"On vacation, are you?"

"You could say that. You could also say I'm mixing business with pleasure. I'm a writer, and at the moment, I'm working on a novel set in a small coastal town in northern California. I drove through Dinsmore a couple years back and thought I'd return to have a closer look around, maybe add a little authenticity to my story."

"You don't say. A writer? What kind of book are you writing?"

"It's a mystery."

"Really?" Gideon asked with a grin. He was very impressed. "Well, isn't that something? I don't read a whole lot, myself, but my wife does. And she *loves* mysteries. I'll have to tell her about this. What's your name?"

"Well, she wouldn't recognize my real name. I write under the pen name of Jamison White."

"Jamison White." Gideon removed his pen and notepad, opened the pad, and handed them both to the man. "Could I get you to write that down?"

"Be glad to."

Gideon laughed. "I guess you could say I'd like your autograph. Just might tickle the heck out of my wife."

The man chuckled as he handed the pad back to Gideon. "Well, I hope you'll give her my best."

"Sure will." Gideon got serious again as he put his notepad away, remembering why he'd stopped the man in the first place. "By the way, where are you staying?"

"At the Dinsmore Cove Inn."

"And . . . that can be verified?"

"Sure. Just call the place."

Gideon nodded.

"Is there something wrong, officer? Do you . . . suspect me of something?"

"Well, we have a boy missing here in town."

"Really? That's awful. I'm sorry to hear it. A child?"

"Teenager. Name's Lenny Cochran. Actually, you want to know what I think, I don't think he's *missing*, really, just ran away for a while. His old man's a nasty drunk. I'd probably run off too." Gideon shrugged. Then he thought that perhaps he'd said too much and should shut his mouth. "Well, Mr. White, I'll let you be off. I'm on my way back to the station to get off my shift."

"Have a good evening, officer."

"Thank you much."

As he got back into his car Gideon reminded himself to call the Dinsmore Inn and ask if a Jamison White was registered, just to be sure. He'd completely forgotten that the man had told him Jamison White was only his *pen* name, not his *real* name, and it never occurred to Gideon that he would not very likely be registered under that name. It didn't matter, though; he never called the inn. By the time he got to the station, he figured there was really no point; the man's story sounded good. Gideon wanted to get home, share the story with his wife, and surprise her with a mystery writer's autograph.

The man who had introduced himself as Jamison White watched Gideon's patrol car drive away, glad that his story had worked. The story was true, of course, but sometimes people weren't too willing to believe it. Unfortunately, he did not carry any copies of his books around with him to serve as identification. It was also true that Jamison White was not his real name, and he was glad that his hunch had proved correct; he'd suspected the police officer would not be *quite* bright enough to pursue it and ask for his *real* name.

He'd lied about one thing, however. He was not in town to do research for a book. He was in town on a search that he'd been on for many years: the search for Wesley Coswell. That search had finally come to an end. He'd found Wesley Coswell. He just didn't know quite what to do about it now. He'd made some steps in the right direction, though, and that was more than he'd ever done before. He knew a number of things about Wesley Coswell . . . enough to wonder if perhaps he was connected to the disappearance of this teenager, Lenny Cochran . . . enough to think that perhaps he should look into Lenny Cochran's disappearance. One of the things he knew abut Wesley Coswell—perhaps the most *important* thing—was the name he was using here in Dinsmore.

Wesley Coswell was Gregory Trancas.

Dinner had been wonderful. The food itself had certainly been nothing special, but it was hot and it was a break from the drudgery of all those assignments he'd been working on that day. But shortly after Lenny was finished eating, Mr. Trancas came in with the binder and a few books tucked under one arm. His expression was stern, somber. He put the books on the nightstand and said, "Enjoy your dinner?"

"Uh-huh."

"Good. Now get up and get in the desk. It's time to go back to work."

The desk. Lenny stared at it for a long time before getting off the cot and walking over to it. He seated himself cautiously, apprehensively.

"Now," Mr. Trancas said in an impersonal, unfriendly tone of voice that suggested he was getting down to business, "here are the assignments you did. I'd like you to look over them." He put the papers on the desk top, clasped his hands behind his back, and began pacing, waiting for Lenny to do as he was told.

Finally, Lenny looked over the papers.

There were check marks . . . a *lot* of check marks in heavy red ink. He wasn't sure what they meant, but they frightened him. They frightened him so much, in fact, that he couldn't concentrate enough to figure out exactly *what* mistakes he'd made.

"As you can see," Mr. Trancas said, "you have a number of errors there. Many of them are simply the wrong answers. Others are errors in spelling, grammar, and punctuation, which, of course, are just as important as the right answer." Mr. Trancas stopped in front of the desk and leaned forward slightly, touching all ten fingertips to the desk top. "Did I mention earlier that I grade on a pass or fail basis? There is no in between. So, do you know what that means, Leonard?" he asked quietly.

The gentle, curious tone of his voice terrified Lenny so much that he was unable to respond. He simply stared up at the teacher.

"That means you failed and you must be disciplined. Because discipline is the best teacher of all. So I will tell you how I handle discipline."

He began pacing again, now with his arms folded over his chest.

"Do you see the cables hanging over your head?"

Lenny didn't even have to look up. His insides turned to ice.

When Mr. Trancas noticed that Lenny was not looking overhead, he smiled. "Of course, you already know about them. You took *pictures* of them. You're aware of the manacles on the ends of the cables. Aren't you?" He stopped, waiting for a response.

Lenny nodded his head.

"Good. *That* is how I handle discipline." He stopped again, hovering over the desk. Reaching overhead with both hands, he grasped the manacles and pulled the cables down with a metallic clanking sound.

Lenny stiffened, holding his breath.

Mr. Trancas lifted Lenny's left hand and fastened one of the manacles around his wrist, then began with the other, saying, "For every one of those check marks you got tonight—and every night from now on—you spend five minutes hanging from these manacles suspended over this desk."

A small whining sound escaped Lenny's throat.

"And then you will be strapped into the desk—yes,

that's what the restraints are for, because I'm sure you were wondering—while I lecture you about your mistakes."

The manacles closed with a horribly loud cuh-*lack* . . . cuh-*lack*.

"Is that understood?" Mr. Trancas asked.

Sure that his face was betraying his terror, Lenny nodded, his throat dry and scratchy.

"Don't worry, Lenny. This won't happen often. Not if you're a good student. I've found that this kind of discipline brings tre*mendous* results, and those results do not require discipline. Do you understand?"

Lenny nodded again, jerkily. And then something happened. Something inside of Lenny clicked.

He thought of all the years he'd put up with his father's shouting and slapping and slugging. He thought of all the times he'd wanted to scream at his father, to fight back, to shout at him, *"Stop it!"* But Lenny had never done that because it was his father. It wasn't someone else, it wasn't a stranger, it was his *father*.

But this was someone else, a stranger, and suddenly Lenny could not bring himself to tolerate it the way he'd tolerated abuse from his father for so many years. Suddenly, he found himself incapable of *not* screaming.

So he screamed. He just closed his eyes, leaned back his head, and screamed at the top of his lungs.

He could almost feel Mr. Trancas stiffen. He heard the teacher's breathing quicken, and when he finally opened his eyes, Lenny saw Mr. Trancas's fists clenching and unclenching again and again at his sides. When he ran out of breath, Lenny stopped for just a moment to inhale, then began to scream again.

"All *right*!" Mr. Trancas barked, and his voice was

frightening, rising so easily above Lenny's scream that Lenny stopped abruptly. "I can see you aren't going to make this *easy*!" He rushed across the room to a box against the wall and came back with something in each hand. Moving with lightning speed, he slapped a tennis ball into Lenny's mouth so hard that his teeth ached and pressed a fat strip of electrical tape over it. "Okay, there! How's that? Huh? Is that better? You can't scream now, can you?"

Lenny stared up at the man, breathing rapidly through his nose, his eyes wide with fear.

"Good. Now. Just relax." Mr. Trancas walked to the shadowy corner of the room and stood between the two cranks. Wrapping his fists around the handles, he began to turn them. Slowly.

The cranking sound seemed deafening to Lenny as his arms were raised slowly above his head . . . as the cables tightened and he was lifted gradually from the desk.

Then Lenny began to cry.

EIGHTEEN

THE STRANGER

It had been rainy and windy the night before, and Pamela had lain awake in bed for hours listening to the wind outside and wondering where Lenny was spending the night.

This morning, however, the rain was gone, and the morning was still, covered by a blanket of lazily moving fog that passed over town very slowly, almost as if it were diligently searching for something.

Pamela drove to school alone that morning, parked her car in the lot, and was heading for the building when she heard footsteps hurrying up behind her. She spun around and gasped when she saw a tall man in a dark overcoat and rain hat with a black patch over his left eye hurrying toward her. He slowed his pace suddenly and smiled.

There's word out about a stranger who's been hanging

around town, Officer Gideon had said yesterday. *A tall man with an eyepatch.*

"Excuse me, miss. I didn't mean to frighten you. I just wanted to catch you before you rushed off."

"Who . . . a-are you?" she stammered.

"My name is Edward Coswell. Ed. And . . . who are you?"

"I'm . . . Laura," she lied, still cautious. "What can I do for you?"

"Well, Laura, I'm curious to know if you're in any of Mr. Trancas's classes."

That made her flinch. "Why?"

"I'm . . . curious."

"But *why* are you curious? I don't know you. You don't work at the school. I've never seen you before. Why should you want to know if I'm in Mr. Trancas's class? Do you even know him?"

"Well, yes. As a matter of fact, I do."

"And does he know you? I mean, if I tell him I've been talking to Edward Coswell, will he know who I'm talking about?"

The man thought a moment, chewed on his lips, looked away from Pamela, and seemed to debate whether or not to speak. Then: "Yes, he'd know. But I hope you don't do that. Mr. Trancas is not who he says he is, and he might very well hurt you if you do that." He stopped again, closed his eyes and seemed to regret what he'd just said. "I'm sorry. That was . . . I'm . . . I'm nobody, miss. I'm . . . no, I don't know Mr. Trancas. Forget what I've told you, and . . . please, have a nice day." He turned quickly and started to walk away.

For a moment, Pamela just stared at his back, feeling cold and stiff and scared for *different* reasons now.

Mr. Trancas is not who he says he is, and he might very well hurt you . . . he might very well hurt you . . . hurt you . . .

Everything Lenny had said to her about Mr. Trancas suddenly came back in a rush, and she was sick for not taking him seriously . . . at least a *little* more seriously. She *had* to know what that man was talking about. She couldn't let him get away.

"Sir!" she called, hurrying after him.

He stopped and turned. "Yes?"

Hesitantly, she asked, "What did you mean . . . about Mr. Trancas hurting me?"

The man in the eyepatch didn't answer, but just waved and walked away.

At the end of the first period, Pamela headed straight for Mr. Elliot's office, even though she didn't have an appointment, and even though she would be late for, or perhaps even miss, her second-period class.

"What can I do for you, Pamela?" Mr. Elliot asked. He looked a little distracted at first, as if he were surprised to see her so suddenly at this time of day, but after a moment, he took on an expression of concern and gestured for her to take a seat.

"Well, Mr. Elliot, I'm not sure. Sorry to bother you, I . . . I just felt I needed someone to talk to."

"About?"

"Lenny."

"Ah. Lenny again." He didn't sound skeptical or annoyed, but understanding. "What about him?"

"He's disappeared."

Mr. Elliot's smile fractured and fell away. "I'm sorry?"

"He's gone. He didn't come to school yesterday, but he wasn't in his room when his parents woke up. He's just . . . gone. They've notified the police, and they're looking, but so far, he hasn't shown up. I called Mrs. Cochran again this morning, and they still haven't heard from him."

He leaned forward, propped an elbow on his desk top, and frowned. After remaining silent for a long time, he said, "Do you have any idea where he might have gone?"

"No. I went with some friends to look for him last night, but we didn't find him—obviously. We think maybe he took off because he had a big fight with his dad the night before. But . . . there's more. There was a man in the parking lot this morning. He stopped me on my way in. He was wearing an eyepatch. Officer Gideon mentioned him yesterday at the Cochrans. He said he'd look into this guy to find out if he might have something to do with Lenny's disappearance. But today, this man—he says his name is Edward Coswell—he wanted to know if I was in Mr. Trancas's class. I was suspicious of him, so I didn't say much. In fact, I got a little upset and said he probably didn't know Mr. Trancas at all, and I'd tell Mr. Trancas that an Edward Coswell was hanging around asking questions about him. He said that wouldn't be a good idea because Mr. Trancas wasn't who he *said* he was and might hurt me. Then, all of a sudden, he totally denied that he knew Mr. Trancas, and he told me I should just forget what he'd said. But I thought of all the things Lenny had said, and I thought maybe they weren't so crazy after all. I got really scared." Pamela paused and bowed her head, embarrassed. "I'm not sure why, I just . . . suddenly

I knew something wasn't right, and I turned and hurried away. And now . . . well, I don't know if I did the wrong thing or . . . or . . . well, I just don't know." She fidgeted in her chair as she took a deep, tremulous breath.

Mr. Elliot pursed his lips, tapped his chin with his forefinger thoughtfully, and was silent for a while. Then he asked, "You say the police officer mentioned this man with the eyepatch?"

"Mm-hm," she said with a nod.

Again he was quiet for a while. "Look, Pamela, you have a class to get to if I'm not mistaken. Why don't you do that. I'll take care of this. I'm very glad you came to me. Don't worry about it for now. I'm sure Lenny is fine. From what you told me about his home life, I wouldn't be surprised if he just wanted to get away from his father. But I'll talk to all the right people—the authorities, for one—if I think this information will help. In the meantime, you have things to do." He smiled and stood. "So why don't you get to them."

She stood, too, tried to smile, and said so long. But as she headed for her next class several thoughts ran through her mind. She thought she'd made a mistake; she wished none of this had ever happened to her so her life could go on smoothly; but most of all, she wondered about Lenny, and if he was all right, and if maybe he'd known something all along that no one *else* had known, and, if so . . . how could he possibly be all right?

Mr. Elliot sat at his desk, ignoring his work, and thought for a long time.

If what Pamela said was true, then something was

wrong. Even if it *wasn't* true, something needed to be done about this mysterious stranger. But before he did anything, he felt he needed to talk to Mr. Trancas again. But not at school. He would go see Mr. Trancas at home after school was out.

NINETEEN

MR. ELLIOT'S VISIT

Lenny was hanging from the cables again. The tennis ball was stuffed in his mouth covered with a fat strip of tape.

When Mr. Trancas got home that day, he'd made a sandwich for Lenny, taken the assignments he'd done, and gone upstairs. Shortly before Lenny was finished with his sandwich, as he sat at the school desk, Mr. Trancas returned looking very grim, and for a moment, Lenny thought the sandwich might come right back up.

"You didn't do as well as I'd hoped, Lenny," Mr. Trancas said somberly.

His mouth suddenly dry, Lenny said, "Well, Mr. Trancas . . . those assignments are, um, a little . . . ahead of me . . . I think. And I'm just, um . . . doing the best I can . . . you know?"

He frowned. "Ahead of you? What kind of attitude is that? A true seeker of knowledge would never say such a thing."

"But Mr. Trancas . . . I'm not a genius. I just want . . . y'know, an education, not . . ." But he didn't finish because the look on Mr. Trancas's face was becoming angry.

He came toward Lenny and leaned over him until their faces were very close. Mr. Trancas curled his lips up into a hideous sneer and repeated Lenny's words mockingly in a pinched, whining voice: "But Mr. Trancas, I'm not a genius. I just want, y'know, an education, y'know, y'know, y'know?" He stared at Lenny hatefully for a long time, his twisted lips pressed together, breathing hard through his nose, then said, "That attitude . . . is unacceptable! You are going to be disciplined, Leonard. And *I* am going to go for a brisk walk to work off my frustration, because I'm very frustrated with you right now. And when I get back, we are going to work, do you understand me? We are going to work hard!"

And then Mr. Trancas hung Lenny from the cables and left.

His head hung low between his shoulders, and he stared at the half-eaten sandwich on the desk top. It wasn't long afterward that Lenny heard a sound . . . a *voice*.

He began screaming.

Mr. Elliot rang Mr. Trancas's doorbell.

When there was no response, he rang again. The front door was open and, cupping his hands around his eyes, he pressed them against the outer glass door and peered inside. "Hello? Mr. Trancas?" he called.

Still no response. He started to turn and leave, but at

the last instant, acting on an impulse, he tried the door. It opened. Tossing a self-conscious glance over his shoulder, Mr. Elliot stepped into the house.

"Hello?" he called. "Anybody home?" Silence. He called again, louder, *"Hello?"*

And then he heard it. A small sound, a voice . . . well, something *like* a voice. He couldn't make out what the voice was saying—if it was saying anything at all—but it was impossible to mistake the *tone* of the voice.

Someone was in trouble.

"Is someone here?" Mr. Elliot shouted, then waited for a moment.

The muffled voice responded, and Mr. Elliot went in the direction from which it had seemed to come.

"Hello? Are you . . . all right?"

He went through the living room cautiously, feeling a little guilty at first for just walking into Mr. Trancas's house so boldly, but when he started through the dining room and heard the voice again—closer this time and brimming with terror—he thought it was probably a good thing he had. He rushed into the kitchen, expecting to find the source of the voice, but found only a cockatoo.

"Craw-*craawwwk*! Oh, my gosh! Oh, my gosh!"

Mr. Elliot sighed, relieved for only a moment. Then he heard the voice again, an unintelligible ragged scream. It was coming from beyond the door beneath the birdcage.

Suddenly Mr. Elliot was overwhelmed by a feeling of horrible dread. His hand trembled as he turned the knob. He looked down the staircase, took four cautious steps toward the basement, and gasped when he saw two legs hanging limply above a school desk.

"Oh, my *God*!" he hissed as he rushed down the stairs.

He stood on the cement floor for a long time, mouth hanging open as he stared at Lenny Cochran hanging from the manacles above the desk. "Lenny, what . . . how . . . did Mr. Trancas . . ."

Lenny began to scream again, his voice muffled by the ball and the tape over his mouth. He screamed so hard, his face turned blood red.

"I . . . I don't know how to get you down, Lenny," Mr. Elliot said. But of course, Lenny was unable to reply. So, Mr. Elliot went to him, moved the desk over, and climbed up on the chair to get to the tape. As he was pulling at a corner of it Lenny's eyes got even wider, and he began to scream again . . . again and again, his eyes rolling in his head. Mr. Elliot ripped the tape off, pried the ball from Lenny's mouth, and at that instant, Lenny screamed.

"Behind you behind you behi—"

Mr. Elliot looked over his shoulder just in time to see the harsh light from overhead glint off the blade of the knife in Mr. Trancas's hand. Then all he felt was agonizing pain.

Mr. Trancas stood over Mr. Elliot's body for a long time, the knife clutched in his fist. Then he looked up at Lenny and said in a tremulous voice, "That's what I get for not locking the door when I go for a walk."

TWENTY

THE STRANGER'S STORY

"Something's wrong," Pamela said. "I don't care if it *does* sound crazy, something weird is going on here. First, Mr. Lehman disappears, then turns up dead. *Murdered.* Then Lenny disappears. *After* he's tried to tell me that there's something strange about Mr. Trancas and that he's been snooping around Mr. Trancas's house. Then Mr. Elliot disappears."

"He didn't disappear," Dave said, sitting across from her at the Burger Barrel. "He just didn't show up at school yesterday."

"Wrong," Pamela snapped. "He left right after classes ended yesterday, but he didn't take his stuff with him. His briefcase, his papers, even his checkbook. And he told the receptionist in the counseling office that he was going to see Mr. Trancas and he would be back in a while."

"Where did you hear this?" Teresa asked.

"From Mrs. Oliver. The receptionist in the counseling office. She's a good friend of my mother's, and we talk sometimes. She tells me things. And she said Mr. Elliot said he'd be back in a while. But he *didn't* come back. And he didn't come back *today*, either."

"So what're you saying?" Todd asked. "What do you think is wrong?"

"I don't know."

Charlene asked, "You think what Lenny said was true? About Mr. Trancas being a killer?"

"I don't *know*." Pamela paused, then looked at each of them sitting at the booth and said quietly and *very* seriously, "But who's to say it's not?"

"It is true," said the man sitting in the next booth behind David and Charlene as he turned around and looked between them at Pamela. He wore a black eye-patch over his left eye.

Pamela gasped.

"He *is* a killer," the man said quietly, calmly. "And his name is not Gregory Trancas. It's Wesley Coswell. He's my brother."

They invited him to their booth, but only after Pamela persuaded them. She was suddenly interested in what he had to say, somehow certain that it was connected to Lenny's disappearance as well as Mr. Elliot's . . . even if she *hadn't* convinced her friends that Mr. Elliot had disappeared.

They took on different expressions, however, when Edward Coswell began to tell his story.

"Our father was a college history professor—very intelligent and very demanding. Maybe it *is* true that there's a fine line between genius and insanity. If so, our father straddled it, and he probably pushed Wesley over that line. You see, our father was a very sick man—mentally ill. He physically abused both Wes and me, though Wes got the worst of it. I think my father just didn't like the fact that his son was actually as intelligent as he, maybe even smarter. Maybe he felt intimidated—threatened—by Wesley. Whenever he got into a hostile fit, he always took out most of his anger on poor Wes."

Coswell waved a waitress over to the table and ordered a cup of coffee.

"After so many years of being physically and mentally beaten, my brother just went over the edge. All of those years that we were growing up, Wes couldn't understand why Dad did that to him. He never told anyone about it, but he confided to me that he felt like he was being punished. He just couldn't understand it—most parents wanted their kids to do well in school, but for some reason it was like our father didn't." Coswell sighed heavily and rubbed his eyes.

"As I said, our father was a very sick man, and now I'm afraid my brother has become an even sicker man."

Coswell stopped talking as the waitress came with his coffee. He nodded his thanks to her and took several quick sips before he continued.

"I can't even describe what we went through. The reason I wear this—" He pointed to his eyepatch. "—is because my father once hit me a little too hard. But I was the lucky one. What he did to my brother didn't leave any visible scars, but it destroyed him emotionally."

Coswell sipped his coffee again, remaining silent.

Pamela's mouth was dry. Coswell's story was terrifying her, and a glance around the table told her the others felt the same. She took a sip of ice water, then whispered, "What are you trying to tell us, Mr. Coswell?"

Coswell started speaking in a slow, measured voice. "It's difficult to talk about all of this, especially with strangers. But to be completely honest, I'm afraid for you. Wes and I drifted apart years ago. I'd been pressuring him to get medical help because it was obvious that I couldn't help him work through his problems. Maybe Wes felt too pressured—one day he left, disappeared without a trace. After years of trying to track him down, I finally found him in Wyoming, although I didn't have a chance to speak to him. He seemed to disappear from there as quickly as he'd left home. I've followed him for some time, and I'm now certain that he's been involved in some horrible crimes. As much as I love my brother and want to protect him, I know I have to expose him."

Coswell paused. He was nervously folding his napkin into small, neat pleats. Finally he looked up and glanced around the group, his eyes resting on Pamela.

"Look, you must believe me. Wes is sick. He wants to make other students suffer the way he has. The student he chooses could be one of you. Or one of your friends."

Pamela's skin crawled. She said, "I think he's already made his choice."

Coswell listened closely as Pamela shared with him everything that Lenny had told her. She just hoped it wasn't too late.

When Pamela was finished, Dave asked Coswell, "Look, why don't you just go to the police?"

"I've tried that before," he said. "In other towns. But it doesn't work. Wes never uses the same name twice, and he does a wonderful job of hiding his identity."

"But you've got something solid now," Pamela said. "We know that Lenny has disappeared, and he's been telling me about Mr. Trancas—about your brother—all along!"

Coswell glanced away from them, almost guiltily. "Well," he said, "it's not that easy. I can't just go to the police. See, I . . ." He looked at Pamela again. "I killed my father."

Coswell looked around at the shocked and wary faces surrounding him. He started to speak again, but now his voice was nervous and his words were fast.

"It was a particularly violent scene one night in our house. My father was beating up on Wes, screaming and yelling at him, and I was secretly watching from upstairs. I guess something snapped—all I know is that I couldn't take it anymore. I had this old rusted hunting knife hidden in my closet. That night I dug it out and used it—on my father. The stab didn't kill him. It was the shock of being hit from behind—and probably the stress of constant fighting—that caused him to die from a massive heart attack."

There was a long pause, tense as a taut rubber band, as Coswell stared at his coffee, and the others stared at him, occasionally exchanging glances with one another. The man they were sitting with, their eyes seemed to be saying, had actually *killed* someone.

"My mother probably felt that my father got his just reward. In fact, I think she was glad—relieved—that I killed him, that at least he'd never hurt us again. My mother helped me escape before the police came.

"I've been wanted by the FBI ever since. I've been searching for my brother after first finding him in Wyoming and then reading the newspaper articles about those murdered teens. Now my worst fears are confirmed."

"What are we going to do about Lenny? We have to help him!" Pamela cried.

"Yes," Coswell said solemnly. "We have to get to Lenny."

"So what are we going to do?" Teresa snapped.

Coswell finished his coffee, then stood and said, "I'll take care of it."

"But shouldn't we go to the police?" Todd asked.

"For my sake, please don't," Coswell said.

"But what about Lenny's sake?" Pamela asked.

Standing beside the table, Coswell put his hand on Pamela's shoulder and said softly, "If my brother has kidnapped your friend, and if he's okay, I promise I'll get him out by tonight."

TWENTY-ONE

THE REUNION

"Well, Lenny, I have to tell you." Mr. Trancas dragged a chair over and sat down beside the cot with a manila folder in his lap. "You've disappointed me. Greatly. I'm especially disappointed in your performance in English. I thought you wanted to be a writer."

By this time, Lenny was terrified. Each time Mr. Trancas came into the room, Lenny's entire body stiffened in anticipation of what was to come. He was no longer able to control the expression on his face; his mouth became dry, his eyes widened, and he began to tremble all over. He was doing all those things now as he stared up at Mr. Trancas. He was tied to the cot at his wrists and ankles and lay perfectly still as Mr. Trancas stared down at him sternly.

"Did you hear me, Lenny? I said, I thought you wanted to be a writer."

"Yes, yes, I do, I *do* want to be a writer."

Mr. Trancas swung the folder through the air in front of Lenny's face. "With grades like *this*?"he shouted.

"But grades don't have anything to do with being a writer, and besides . . . the grades I got in school are-are . . . they're *good*, I mean, I don't under—"

"But that's in *school*! You're not in school anymore. You're *here*!" He stood, his eyes fiery, and pointed an angry finger at Lenny, shouting, "This is *not* Dinsmore High School! This is my basement! This is the School of Thought! Remember that I'm your *only* teacher now! I'm your *principal* now!" He leaned so close that Lenny could feel and smell his hot breath when he hissed, "This isn't just *school* anymore! This . . . is . . . an *education*!"

Lenny felt Mr. Trancas's spittle on his face as the man roared the last word. When he spoke again, Mr. Trancas's voice was a hot, angry whisper.

"Now, Lenny. Tell me. Does that sound important to you?"

"Important?"

"Is there something wrong with your ears? Are you not hearing well today? I asked you if an education is important. So. *Is* it?"

"Well, yes. It's important."

"Then why aren't you trying harder?" He spoke quietly, calmly, but there was an ominous undertone to his voice.

When Lenny spoke, his voice was little more than a weak breath. "I . . . *am* . . . trying harder."

"Then why isn't it *working*?"

"Leave the boy alone."

The voice from the stairs made Mr. Trancas jump and spin around, and when he did, he gasped, "Oh, my God."

Lenny looked up and saw the man he'd seen in the parking lot a few days ago—the man with the eyepatch—standing at the top of the stairs, looking sternly at Mr. Trancas.

"Edward?" Mr. Trancas whispered, a smile spreading over his face slowly. "Eddie? Is that you?"

"Yes, it's me, Wes."

"Oh, my God, Eddie. I can't believe it," Mr. Trancas hissed through an enormous grin. "It's so . . . so very good to see you!" They stared at each other for a long time, Mr. Trancas grinning, while the other man stared daggers at him.

"Leave the boy alone, Wesley," the man on the stairs said calmly, quietly.

But Mr. Trancas seemed oblivious of the man's words. He walked away from Lenny's side slowly, staring up at the man, smiling.

Wes? Lenny thought. ***Why is he calling him Wes?***

"But, Eddie," Mr. Trancas whispered, "it's been so *long*."

"I know, Wes. And we can talk and catch up all you want. Just . . . leave the boy alone, all right?"

Mr. Trancas began to nod, still smiling. "Yes, yes, okay, if that's what you want. Would you like to talk? Would you like to—well, we can step outside, Eddie. How's that? We can go upstairs and go talk on the back porch. Does that sound all right? I'd like that."

The man on the stairs looked at Lenny for a long time, as if to determine whether or not Lenny was okay. Then he turned his gaze to Mr. Trancas and nodded. "All right, Wes. That would be nice."

The man's voice sounded so . . . so *fake* to Lenny. But Lenny said nothing, just watched the two men as Mr. Trancas turned to him and said, "I'll be back in a while, Leonard. I'm going to visit with my brother." Then he turned and headed up the stairs.

Both men left the basement, and the door closed solidly behind them.

Lenny closed his eyes, trying not to tremble.

Wes Coswell led his brother across the kitchen, heading for the back door.

"Why do we have to go outside, Wes?" Ed asked. "Can't we just take a seat in here and talk?" He was uncertain about his brother's intentions, nervous about the way Wes was staring at him as Wes backed toward the door.

"Why inside?" Wes asked. "The clouds are starting to clear up, there's still plenty of sunlight. Wouldn't you like to sit out on the patio and talk? It's been so *long*, Eddie. We have so much to talk about . . . so much to say . . ." His smile never wavered, and his eyes twinkled with an almost childlike glee.

Ed stared at him for a long time. Something about it didn't quite sit right with him, but he didn't want to antagonize Wes. He'd come without any particular plan in mind, and now, as he stood in the kitchen, he began to wonder if he'd made a mistake. Yes, he *could* have gone to the police, and yes, they *would* have slapped cuffs on him as soon as they realized who he was—if, in fact, they recognized him at all—but wouldn't that have been a better way to stop it?

Without even thinking about what he was going to say, Ed spoke: "Why, Wesley? How could you do it? After what Dad put us through all those years, how could you do this?"

Finally, Wes's smile faded slowly, and he stopped moving toward the door. He just stood there, staring at Ed, his brow gradually furrowing until a dark frown hooded his eyes. "What do you mean . . . after what he *did* to us?" Wes breathed, lips curling ever so slightly into a sneer. "He was a good father." His voice began to rise. "He was the most brilliant man I ever, *ever* knew, and I won't stand here and—" He stopped abruptly and spun away from Ed, going to the counter. Turning his back to his brother, Wes hunched his shoulders and leaned forward on the edge of the counter, taking a deep breath.

Ed felt tense. He'd never seen Wes like this. *He must really be insane,* Ed thought. *He's totally crazy—and violent too.*

Ed's expression must have shown sheer terror, because when Wes spoke again, his voice was calm and the smile returned.

"I'm sorry," Wes said. "Please. Let's go out on the porch and talk. Would you like a soda? Some coffee, perhaps?"

Ed shook his head no and followed Wes to the back door . . . out onto the patiolike back porch. He got only a glimpse of the monstrous Doberman before his brother shouted, "*Kill*, Teddy!"

And then Ed's field of vision was filled with nothing but

two rows of flashing yellowed fangs and black flaring nostrils.

Lenny flinched when the basement door was suddenly kicked open. He looked up and saw Mr. Trancas backing in, his arms hooked under the arms of the other man as he dragged him down the stairs. The man's limp feet clumped on each step; he was bloody and his clothes were torn, but he appeared to be alive.

Mr. Trancas dragged him to the school desk and propped him up in the seat, fastening the straps around his chest and waist, leaving his arms free. He looked at Lenny. His face was twisted, angry, and his shoulders heaved with each breath.

"You've turned out to be a great disappointment, Leonard," he said, voice trembling. "I'm afraid this isn't going to work. Taking you on was a mistake. You've been much more trouble than you're worth. I think I'll have to expel you."

"Ex . . . expel me?"

"That's right. Look at all the trouble you've caused." He gestured toward the man at the desk. "This fellow . . . my own *brother*," he hissed in disbelief. "Your counselor at school, Mr. Elliot. There are other students far more worthy of this opportunity than you, Leonard, students who would be thrilled to receive such individual attention, such superior training in the arts and sciences. Students who wouldn't be so much *trouble*. I'm afraid your stay here has come to an end."

Lenny felt his insides clutch with fear, and he tried to speak, unsuccessfully at first, then with a frightened stammer: "I-I-I'm sorry M-Mr. Trancas. I'll try harder, I p-promise. I'll study harder and do b-better."

Mr. Trancas studied him for a long moment, then shook his head. "No, I'm afraid not. It's too late. It would be a waste of time for both of us." He turned and started up the stairs, pausing for a moment to look at the bloodied man slumped at the desk. "I'll take care of both of you," he said as he opened the door. "Later . . ."

Terrified, Lenny began to tremble uncontrollably.

TWENTY-TWO

PAMELA GETS WORRIED

Pamela had been unable to eat her dinner that evening and walked away from the table leaving her plate full.

She couldn't do her homework, couldn't read, couldn't even watch television. Her conscience was eating at her. They should have called the police immediately, no matter what Mr. Coswell wanted. In fact, the more she thought about it, the more it bothered her . . . the more certain she was that they'd made a horrible mistake, one that was, perhaps, too late to correct.

Mumbling an "excuse me" as she left the dining room, she went to her father's office for privacy and called David.

"I'm scared," she said as soon as he answered.

"About what?"

"Well, what do you *think*? About Lenny, that's what. I think we should call the police. Right now."

"But what about Mr. Coswell? He said—"

"Forget about what he said, will you? I'm thinking about Lenny! Why should we trust a total stranger? We know something's wrong, we should go to the police."

"And tell them what? If we don't trust Coswell, why tell them his story? And if we don't tell them his story, we'd just be telling them something they already know—that Lenny's missing."

"Well . . . we should do *something*!"

"But *what*?" David asked, exasperated.

Pamela said nothing, waiting for him to answer his own question.

He sighed, "Okay, okay. Here's what we'll do. Tomorrow, after school, you and I will go over to Mr. Trancas's . . . Mr. Coswell's . . . whatever. We'll make up some excuse—we can ask for help with something, maybe, I don't know—and while we're there, we'll just, you know, feel him out, sort of look around and see what we can see. Sound good?"

"Just the two of us?" she asked doubtfully.

"What do you want to do, take a posse?"

"Well, don't you think it would be a little risky for just the two of us to go? Alone? I mean, what if he . . . suspects something?"

"So, what are you saying, that we take the others? Teresa and Charlene and Todd?"

"Why not?"

"Good grief, Pamela, the guy'll think he's under siege!"

"Well, he's less likely to try anything then, don't you think?"

Another frustrated sigh came over the line.

"*Please*, David," Pamela said quietly. "If I'm wrong,

what harm can it do? Maybe we'll annoy him a little by dropping in, so what? Lenny might be in trouble. For all we know, *Coswell* might be in trouble. After all, he did say he'd have Lenny back by tonight. Well . . . it's tonight already. And I think . . . well, I think we should go over there tonight. Right *now*."

"You're kidding."

"No, I'm not kidding!"

"Well, that's sure not going to work. It's too late. He'd really suspect something if all of us showed up on his doorstep tonight. By the time all of us got together and we got over there, it'd be even later. No, I'm not going to do that. But, look. We'll go over there tomorrow, right after school. By then, Coswell might have Lenny back. If everything he told us was true and Lenny *is* over there, we might screw up whatever Coswell's doing to get him *out* if we go over now."

Pamela sighed loudly, frustrated.

"I know you're worried, but go to bed," David said. "Drink some hot chocolate if you have to, or read a boring book, something that'll put you to sleep. And I *promise* . . . if Coswell doesn't have him back tomorrow, we'll pay Mr. Trancas—*What's*-His-Name—a visit. Okay?"

She sighed again, more quietly this time. She knew it was hopeless to continue trying to convince David to go over to Mr. Trancas's tonight. "All right, David . . . we'll do it tomorrow," she lied. "Good night."

It had been a lie because she had no intention of waiting until tomorrow. She had no intention of waiting for *anything*.

Pamela had decided that she would go over to Mr. Trancas's *tonight* . . . alone.

TWENTY-THREE

LENNY'S EXPULSION

Pamela drove through the rain, trembling.

Occasionally, jagged lightning appeared between the clouds in the distance like giant, crooked fingers of polished, white bone, making her blink; the lightning was nightmarishly distorted through the rain blurring the windshield in spite of the wipers' efforts to keep up with it.

What would she ask Mr. Trancas once she got there? What possible excuse could she use for disturbing him so late in the evening? She was so nervous and upset that she couldn't remember what they were studying in Mr. Trancas's class, so she couldn't *think* of a question for him.

She would be there very soon. She'd looked up his address in the telephone directory. Her entire body shuddered as she turned down his street and began squinting through the rain-streaked glass at the house numbers.

Lenny could hear Mr. Trancas upstairs talking to the bird. The cheerful tone of his voice was frightening.

Coswell was slumped at the desk, nodding in and out of consciousness, his bloody head jerking up now and then, his eyes staring, unfocused, at Lenny. Finally, he began to fight his condition, took a few deep breaths, and spoke.

"I have a gun," he rasped at Lenny as he groped in his coat pocket. He removed his derringer with a trembling hand.

Lenny's eyes widened, and he made a muffled sound behind the tape and tennis ball.

"It's a derringer, so it's only got two shots. They'll . . . have to be used . . . wisely. I didn't want to use it at all, unless . . . it became absolutely . . . necessary. Obviously . . . it's necessary. I'm afraid . . . that it's either him . . . or us." He concealed the little gun within the folds of his coat, never letting go of it, then leaned his head back and closed his eyes, breathing slowly.

Lenny could hear Mr. Trancas upstairs, saying, in a happy voice, "So, how shall we do it, Woodrow? Quick and neat? Slowly . . . to punish them?"

"Craw-*craawwk*! Little monsters! Little monsters!"

"They certainly are, Woodrow. Let's see . . . something neat and quick, I think. Easily cleaned up . . ."

Please let this work, Lenny thought desperately, glancing at Edward. His eyes were still closed, head still back, his breathing slow, as if he were asleep. Lenny made a garbled sound and startled him.

"Don't worry," he rasped. "I'm awake."

They waited, listening to the movement upstairs, to Mr. Trancas's happy voice. He began to whistle. It was a happy tune, something from an old movie musical, Lenny thought.

The door opened, and light spilled down the stairs from the kitchen. He swung it closed and started down into the basement. Lenny saw something dangling from his right hand as he came jauntily down the stairs.

Distant thunder murmured outside.

"I think I'll take care of you first, Lenny," Mr. Trancas said, halfway down the stairs. When he reached the basement's dirty floor, he smiled at the man tied to the desk. "That way, Eddie . . . you get to watch."

He held up his right arm and a three-foot length of rope dangled from his hand. He grasped the free end and pulled the rope taut between both hands threateningly as he turned to Lenny, grinning.

"Leonard," he said quietly, "you're expelled . . ."

The sound of the rain on the roof of the car became louder when Pamela killed the engine in front of Mr. Trancas's house.

No, no, not Mr. Trancas—Wesley Coswell, she thought. *Mr. Trancas doesn't exist. He's just a disguise.* It seemed necessary for her to remind herself of that because she knew she would be facing him in a moment. He would open the door, and she would be standing on his porch and—

What would she say? What would she ask him?

She thought frantically, searching her memory for the subject of their last class, the assignment he'd given. Once it all came back to her, she concocted a suitable question, stared out the rainy window a few moments trying to calm her trembling, then got out of the car and hurried through the downpour, up the walk toward Wesley Coswell's front door.

Lenny stared up with bulging eyes at the approaching rope as its taut fibers grew larger and larger before him, as it came closer and closer. His throat began to feel swollen and constricted before the rope even touched him, his lungs began to burn in anticipation of what he knew would be a slow, torturous death, and he made a strangled mewling sound behind the tennis ball stuffed in his mouth.

Suddenly, there was a loud, explosive pop, as if someone had pulled the string on one of those confetti-filled party favors, and Mr. Trancas simultaneously stiffened and fell forward with a cry of shock and pain. His toupee dropped off, revealing his bald head, shiny with sweat, and it landed on Lenny's face, lying there like some enormous dead insect. Mr. Trancas landed heavily on Lenny's stomach, face-down, knocking the wind from him. He remained there, groaning, long enough for Lenny to see the blood blossoming through his shirt just below his left shoulder, where a tiny hole had been torn by a bullet. Then Mr. Trancas rolled over on his back and climbed to his feet with difficulty, letting go of the rope with his right hand to clutch his left shoulder.

Lenny shook the sweaty toupee from his face and looked at the man at the desk. In his fear, he'd completely forgotten about the gun, which Edward was now pointing wearily, quaveringly, at Mr. Trancas. Edward's brutalized body looked as wilted as an unwatered plant; his eyes were more than half closed, and his bloody head lolled on his neck, as if he were teetering on the edge of unconsciousness.

Growling like an animal, Mr. Trancas moved quickly in spite of his injury, lunging forward and sweeping his foot upward through the air. It caught Edward's wrist sharply, and his unsteady arm shot up, then collapsed limply.

The gun skittered over the concrete floor.

Mr. Trancas stepped forward and clutched his brother's blood-smeared hair in a fist, jerking his head back hard.

"You shouldn't have done that, Eddie," Mr. Trancas sneered through clenched teeth.

Pamela heard the shot and froze halfway up the walk, gasping sharply, her hand slapping over her mouth. Her heart began racing, and her breath quickened as she stared at Wesley Coswell's front door. Suddenly, the ordinary tract house looked ominous, deadly.

She was certain that had been a gunshot.

Fired by whom? *At* whom?

She stood in the rain for what seemed a long time, her hair getting soaked and sticking to her forehead and face in long slick strands. She decided she had to do something. She didn't know *what*, but that, at the moment, seemed unimportant.

Pamela was at the front door in an instant and didn't hesitate to try the knob. It was unlocked. Terrified and soaked, she rushed inside.

Mr. Trancas slapped Edward's bleeding and swollen face with his palm, then swung his arm the other way and backhanded him, jerking his head back and forth again and again. When he finally stopped, he was grinning. With a barely audible chuckle, he reached out and tore the eye-patch from the man's face, clutching his hair again and turning his head toward Lenny, who made another pathetic whimpering sound when he saw the man's eye . . . or, rather, what was left of it.

"Do you see this, Leonard?" Mr. Trancas growled. "This is what happened to my brother, Edward, because he didn't try hard enough. I've given you an opportunity, Leonard . . . an opportunity to learn from a great mind. But you're not trying hard enough either. I have devoted my entire life to learning and passing my knowledge on to students—*true* students who *crave* knowledge—but I will never, *ever* match the mind of Duncan Coswell, our father, the man who tutored my brother and me, as I have tutored you. The man we sorely disappointed. This is what my brother got because he was lazy." Trancas released the man's head and turned to Lenny, smiling. "He was *lucky*."

Just then, the door at the top of the stairs opened, and Lenny's eyes jerked toward the rectangle of light to see a familiar sillhouette.

It was Pamela.

Lenny watched her start down the stairs and shook his head furiously, trying to say, *No! No! Go back! Get out of here!*; but, of course, his words were nothing more than senseless, garbled sound.

"Oh, my God!" Pamela gasped.

Mr. Trancas spun around, snapping, "Who's there?" He looked up the stairs, saw Pamela halfway down the staircase and just stared at her a moment. "Pamela," he finally breathed. "It's you. You've . . . you've *come*!" His voice was soft and gentle, but suddenly ecstatic. "You've come all by yourself!"

Her shoulders were quaking with sobs, and she screamed at Mr. Trancas, *"What have you done? What . . . have you . . . DONE?"*

"Oh, Pamela, please . . . don't be upset with me," Mr. Trancas said imploringly. "Please, come down." He moved slowly around the school desk, his eyes locked onto Pamela, his hand still clutching his bullet wound. "Come down and I will explain. I can explain all of this. And you'll understand. I know that you will understand."

What happened next happened almost too quickly for Lenny to comprehend it. Ed Coswell, still strapped to the school desk, came alive. He lifted his wilted head as his brother walked around behind the desk and along the other side, then ignoring what must have been some very painful wounds—swung around and flung his arms around Mr. Trancas's waist. He and the desk both toppled to the floor heavily. Mr. Trancas grunted, and his head cracked against the concrete; his arms began to flail immediately as he struggled to get out from under his brother and the school desk.

Edward lifted his head with effort, turning to Pamela, and shouted, "The gun! On the floor! Get it! *Now!*"

Pamela stumbled down the stairs hesitantly.

"Now!" Edward panted, his voice slurry and thick. "I can't . . . hold him . . . much longer . . ."

"Where?" Pamela shrieked. "Where *is* it?"

Edward couldn't respond; he was fading rapidly.

Lenny began screaming so loud and hard that his throat felt torn, and he succeeded in getting Pamela's attention. When she looked at him, he directed her to the gun with his eyes, with jerks of his head, until she spotted it on the floor, glinting slightly in a shadowy corner. She threw herself toward the gun as Mr. Trancas finally began to drag himself out from beneath his brother and the desk.

He swung his right arm out.

His hand grasped Pamela's ankle.

She screamed as she fell and landed with her outstretched hand scant inches from the small firearm.

Mr. Trancas began to pull on her leg, dragging her toward him as he removed himself from under the limp, still body of his brother.

Pamela's entire arm trembled, and she groaned as she strained to reach the gun.

Lenny's chest heaved rapidly, and he could feel his heartbeat in his throat. He sat up as far as he could, pulling his restraints taut, *willing* Pamela's hand to reach the derringer, but . . .

It slid farther away as Mr. Trancas wrapped his hand around her knee, fingers digging into her jeans and pulling . . . *pulling* . . .

Suddenly, Pamela did something that shocked Lenny. She heaved herself onto her back, ignoring the gun now. Setting her jaw, she kicked her foot up, catching Mr. Trancas in the face with the sound of a fist pounding a side of raw beef.

Mr. Trancas's head snapped back, then forward, his face slapping onto the concrete.

Then Pamela scrambled over the floor, swept up the derringer, turned on Mr. Trancas, and backed into the corner, holding the gun on him.

But Mr. Trancas was still. He didn't move.

She stood there for a long time, gasping for air, holding the gun on Mr. Trancas between two quivering hands.

Still, he remained silent and motionless.

Lenny began to jerk at his restraints, shouting garbled pleas for Pamela to free him.

She ran to the cot unsteadily and, without letting go of the gun, untied the straps around Lenny's wrists.

He ripped the tape from his face and spat the tennis ball to the floor, where it bounced, then rolled, over to Mr. Trancas, bumping his motionless arm. Lenny drank air into his lungs through his mouth, wiping beads of sweat from his forehead with the back of his hand. He swung his legs over the edge of the cot and sat up, massaging his wrists as he nodded toward Mr. Trancas's brother.

"How is he, do you think?" he asked.

"I don't know. All I know is, we've got to get upstairs and *lock that door*!"

Lenny began to tremble all over—from shock, from an adrenaline rush, or from simple, sweet relief—and he knew that if he stood, his legs would collapse beneath him. "Just a second," he muttered, then bowed his head and buried his face in his hands with his elbows on his thighs.

He felt Pamela's hand reassuringly caress the top of his head, then his shoulder.

When he started to feel a little more sure of himself, he raised his head and gasped.

A figure was rising up behind Pamela . . .

Mr. Trancas.

"Pamela!" Lenny shouted, but that was all he had time to say.

Mr. Trancas grabbed a handful of Pamela's hair and jerked her backward, wrapped his forearm around her throat, and squeezed her neck to his chest hard. Her tongue shot out of her mouth stiffly, and her eyes bulged as she lifted the gun. Mr. Trancas grabbed her wrist and squeezed hard, dug his fingers into her forearm cruelly until her fingers tremulously released the gun. It hit the floor with a clatter, and Mr. Trancas kicked it over the concrete behind him.

Pamela began to make horrible choking sounds, and the color of her face was growing darker rapidly.

Lenny ignored his shakiness and lunged off the cot in the direction of the gun, but Mr. Trancas stuck out his foot and caught Lenny's shin.

The floor swept up to meet him. He landed hard and painfully with his arms outstretched. Without hesitation, he started to crawl toward the gun, which was four or five feet away, but Mr. Trancas's foot slammed down hard on his back, and he leaned heavily on Lenny, pinning him to the floor as Pamela made more sounds, desperate sounds.

Lenny was weakened by fear and held down by the deadly weight of hopelessness as well as by Mr. Trancas's foot.

Then something moved in the shadows up ahead near the gun.

A hand. A bloody, quivering hand. *Edward's* hand. It crept out from behind the toppled school desk, crawling like a crippled spider toward the gun . . . closer and closer . . . the trembling fingers reaching out with tremendous effort, until—

The fingers touched the barrel of the gun, hooked around it, and pushed it hard with surprising strength. It clattered over the concrete, spinning like a top, straight toward Lenny.

He slapped his hand over the gun, stopping it before it could slide out of reach, picked it up, and twisted his back painfully, craning around to look up at Mr. Trancas.

He lifted the gun . . . hesitated . . .

I'm about to shoot a man, Lenny thought sickeningly, not sure he could do it. He didn't want to kill *anyone* . . . not even Mr. Trancas.

He remembered what Edward had told him earlier. *It's a derringer, so it only has two shots . . . two shots . . . two shots . . .*

That meant there was only one bullet left. He didn't want to miss, but he wasn't sure he wanted to *hit* him, either.

Then he saw Pamela's knees collapsing, heard her fighting for breath, for her *life*.

Lenny fired.

EPILOGUE

Lenny opened his eyes to stare up at the white ceiling of a dimly lighted room. He had a spectacular headache, one that was worst in the front part of his head but spread over his entire skull like an angry octopus with powerful steel coils for tentacles.

This isn't my room, he thought. Then: *I wasn't in my room, I was . . . I was in . . .* It took him a while, and he had to think hard to get through the tremendous pain battering the walls of his skull, but it all came back to him finally.

Two faces appeared above him, like blurry alien moons at first; he blinked several times, clearing his vision, and he saw his parents looking down at him.

His mother's face was a splotchy red mask, sticky with old tears.

But the surprising thing was that Dad's was too!

When Lenny had stared at him for too long, frowning, his dad turned and stepped away from the bed, embarrassed. Lenny watched him go into the bathroom and close the door.

"How are you, Lenny?" his mom whispered, taking his hand.

"I'm not so sure yet," he slurred.

"Do you remember what happened to you?"

He winced when he moved his head. "Well, some. But I must've lost something because . . . I don't remember getting here."

"You don't need to worry about that right now." She asked if he was in pain, and he said his head hurt . . . and his arms, especially his wrists. She pushed the call button to summon the nurse and let the staff know that Lenny was conscious.

"What's wrong with Dad?" he whispered.

"He was very worried about you," she said in a tone that suggested it was a silly question.

"No, there's something else, I can tell. He's . . . different."

"Well. . . ." She glanced cautiously toward the bathroom and lowered her voice to a breath. "He hasn't had a drink since you disappeared and . . . well, he's having a tough time. Actually, he had a couple at first, then he got very angry. Not at *me*, though. It was as if he'd gotten angry at the *liquor*. He stood up from his chair, cursing and growling, took his glass and bottle into the kitchen, and threw them both into the sink. He chipped the basin and the kitchen *still* reeks of the booze, but—"

She shrugged and grinned. "—who cares? He's never done *anything* like that before. I asked him what was wrong, and he just said, 'I can't *think*,' over and over, again and again . . .

"Please," she whispered, squeezing his shoulder, "go easy on him."

Dad came out of the bathroom and approached the bed hesitantly.

"I'm glad you're okay," he said in a hoarse, unsteady voice. "We were, um . . . pretty worried."

"Thanks, Dad." Lenny tried to smile, but it hurt too much.

"Soon as he's out of the hospital," Dad said, "that teacher's goin' to jail. To *prison*. We'll see to that."

Lenny noticed that his dad's hands were trembling.

"So . . . Trancas is okay?"

Dad smirked. "You shot him in the butt, son. Bullet went right into his hip bone. He's okay, but . . . he isn't too happy right now." He paused, then added, "Because you did that, your friend's still alive. So's that other fellow . . . the teacher's brother." He put his quaking hand on Lenny's and said hoarsely, "Did good, kiddo."

Lenny couldn't remember the last time his dad had called him kiddo. It made Lenny feel good, like a little kid again, without a care or worry on earth.

The nurse came in then, and Mom and Dad stepped out to get lunch in the hospital cafeteria, promising to return soon; then the nurse gave him a shot to help the pain in his throbbing, bandaged head, and in a few minutes, Lenny drifted off to sleep again.

* * *

He awoke—he wasn't sure how much later—to Pamela's smiling face.

"So, how does it feel to be a hero?" she asked. "You know, you're going to be in the newspapers and on television all *over* the place."

His head still hurt, but not as bad as before. He returned her smile. "And you didn't believe me," he whispered. "None of you."

Her smile crumbled as she sat on the edge of the bed and took his hand. "I'm sorry, Lenny. Really. I can't apologize enough. But you have to admit it *was* a pretty farfetched story."

"I know. I don't blame you for not believing me."

There was an awkward pause, then Pamela started telling him about Mr. Trancas's true identity, about what had happened to him and his brother Ed and how it had scarred them both, each in a different way.

"We *should* have believed you, Lenny," she said. "*I* should have, anyway, of all people. Sure it sounded crazy, but so did Jonestown and Ted Bundy. I really am sorry."

He squeezed her hand. "You didn't have a *reason* to believe me. Not after all the tricks I'd played on you guys . . . after all the stories I'd told you, all the times I'd fooled you. I know *I* wouldn't have believed me if I were you." He smirked sheepishly.

"Yeah . . . I thought, at first, that your Mr. Trancas story was just another joke. But you kept getting more and more serious about it. More serious than you'd ever been before about any of the others. I should've known. Sooner, I mean. Maybe before . . . before Mr. Elliot—"

"Oh, I don't know," he interrupted her with a sigh, not wanting to think about that. "I *have* gotten pretty good at those things, you know. I've become pretty accomplished at entertaining you guys." He leaned his head back on the pillow and closed his eyes for a moment. He was still a little rummy from the shot the nurse had given him earlier. When he opened his eyes again, Pamela was frowning at him curiously, head cocked to one side.

"Entertaining us?" she asked, puzzled.

"Yeah. Y'know . . . the jokes, the stories, my scrapbook, my . . . my *raison d'être.*"

"Your *what*? Sounds like some kind of French underwear."

"My *raison d'être*. That's French for 'reason for existence.' "

Her frown deepened, and she stood up from the bed, a little indignantly. *"What?"*

"Well, the reason I can hang around with you guys, I mean. You especially. I mean, I'm not exactly one of you, y'know? I'm not . . . one of the *in* people, one of the popular kids. You know what I mean."

"Like hell I know what you mean!" She was angry now. "You think the only reason we have you around is so you can *entertain* us? Like some kind of-of-of . . . some kind of *court jester*?"

Shocked by her anger, he didn't respond, just stared up at her.

"Well? You really *think* that?"

Hesitantly, he nodded. "Yeah. I mean . . . well, that's what I figured."

"Well, you figured *wrong*, Leonard Cochran." She sat on the bed again, but stiffly now. "We hang around you because we enjoy your company. We *care* about you. Well . . . I can't speak for the others, but I think I'm right.

I *know* I'm right. And I *can* speak for my*self*!" Her voice softened, her anger disappeared, and she smiled. She thought carefully for a moment, as if choosing her words. "I know that *I* care for you. Very, *very* much. I'm just sorry it took all of this for me to finally realize just how much I care for you."

Lenny felt himself blushing as they spent a long moment just looking at one another silently. Then Pamela leaned forward and touched her lips to his gently. The kiss lingered, warm and soft. Then she sat up, smiling, and stroked his face.

Suddenly, Lenny's headache felt much, much better.

Sweet Goodbyes

A wonderful series of heart-rending stories that will make you cry. Ordinary high-school girls are suddenly forced to cope with a life-threatening illness. Things will never be the same again, as each girl fights to survive...

Please Don't Go
Losing David
Life Without Alice
My Sister, My Sorrow
Goodbye, Best Friend
The Dying of the Light

All at £2.99

Order Form

To order direct from the publishers, just make a list of the titles you want and fill in the form below:

Name ....

Address ....

....

....

Send to: Dept 6, HarperCollins Publishers Ltd, Westerhill Road, Bishopbriggs, Glasgow G64 2QT.

Please enclose a cheque or postal order to the value of the cover price, plus:

UK & BFPO: Add £1.00 for the first book, and 25p per copy for each addition book ordered.

Overseas and Eire: Add £2.95 service charge. Books will be sent by surface mail but quotes for airmail despatch will be given on request.

A 24-hour telephone ordering service is avail-able to Visa and Access card holders: 041-772 2281